When Melanie received a postcard from Venice saying, "Wish you were here!" she decided to take Ben Ferguson at his word!

However, before she has been in Venice many hours, she becomes involved in a crime, which makes headline news; a crime which brings her into contact with Carlo Benvenuto, handsome policeman with a roving eye; with Peter Somerville, an equally handsome doctor and his pretty blonde travelling companion; with sordid crime and heartwarming romance.

Venice, entrancing city of lagoons, makes a fascinating background for a fast-moving tale of intrigue, suspense and love.

HELLO,
MY LOVE

by

Daisy Thomson

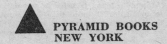
PYRAMID BOOKS
NEW YORK

HELLO, MY LOVE

A PYRAMID BOOK

Published by arrangement with Robert Hale & Company

© D.H. Thomson 1972.
Pyramid edition published February 1974

ISBN 0-515-03291-3

Printed in the United States of America

Pyramid Books are published by Pyramid Communications, Inc. Its trademarks, consisting of the word "Pyramid" and the portrayal of a pyramid, are registered in the United States Patent Office.

Pyramid Communications, Inc., 919 Third Avenue, New York, N.Y. 10022

Hello, My Love

Chapter One

I LOOKED out across the moonlit waters of the Canale di San Marco, and clearly against the nightcloth of the silver sky, as if it were riding on the silver waters of the lagoon, I could see the shimmering, almost unreal outline of the island of San Giorgio Maggiore.

Below me, along the length of the Riva degli Schiavonni, the lights, in their quadra-headed lamp holders seemed to have been extinguished by the very intensity of the moonlight, which caressed the sweeping lines of the black, high-prowed gondolas which were tossing rhythmically at their mooring alongside the quay.

There was a quality of unreality about the scene, as if it was merely part of a dream, a waking hallucination, for even now, twenty-four hours after I had made my spur of the moment decision to fly out to Venice, I still could hardly believe the fact that I was here, in an opulent hotel bedroom in one of the world's most beautiful cities and not dreaming in my little flat in Edinburgh.

One thing convinced me of the reality of the situation. The heat. Edinburgh, even in May-time, would never have been so oppressively hot in the early hours of the morning that I had to fling off all the bedcovers, and was even now contemplating which window to open wide, in spite of the supposed air conditioning, to let what must surely be the cooler night air into a bedroom whose heavy velvet drapes and thick pile carpet seemed to have absorbed the heat of the day and were now discharging it again like well regulated storage heaters.

I had not previously opened the windows, for fear of mosquitoes, but now I was wondering which would be the lesser of two evils—the almost suffocating heat or the misery of a bite from an insect to whose poison I am allergic.

I sat up in bed, hugging my knees, still undecided what to do.

My bedroom was right at the corner of the hotel, and was large, high-ceilinged, and decorated in a style which, with its richly coloured drapes and plush furnishings was, to my mind, uniquely Venetian. It had two windows. The main one, high and wide, opened out onto a minute, wrought iron balcony, which overlooked the Riva and the lagoon. The other, smaller window was a few paces away from my bed, on the right, and faced, as I had noted on my arrival before nightfall, the starkly blank red brick wall of the neighboring building, from which it was separated by a rio leading from the main canal, and which at best was little more than two gondola breadths wide.

After due reflection I decided that this would be the better window to open, since an open window on the first floor, with a convenient balcony for easy access, would be like a direct invitation to any sneak thief who happened to be on the prowl this moonlight night.

It wasn't that I had much of value with me, but I certainly did not relish the thought of waking up and finding an unwanted intruder in my room!

I sighed sleepily and slithered from the bed, making no attempt to switch on the light, since this would only serve to attract the insects I disliked into the room when I opened the window.

The right side of the bedroom was not illuminated by the moonlight which streamed in through the french window at the front, and I stubbed my toe painfully against the leg of the luggage table as I groped my way windowwards, and pulled back the drapes.

In complete contrast to the fairy view from the main window, I found myself looking out into darkness so intense that the narrow rio beneath and the building opposite merged into one great blob of blackness, and only the soft rippling wash of the wavelets against the wall of the hotel betrayed the presence of the water below me.

I stood for a few seconds at the open window, breathing in the night air which, even although it had an indefinable, not entirely pleasant odour, which was a mixture of mouldering dampness and decay, with a soupçon of fumes from the motorboats and other craft which plied busily along it during the day, and more than a soupçon of the smells of cooking from the kitchen which was almost directly under my room, was at least cooler and less oppressive than the musty heat of velvet and thick carpet which pervaded the bedroom.

As I stood there, my eyes began to grow accustomed to the darkness, and I thought I could discern a definite shape among the stable shadows, as if a high prowed gondola was moving towards me from the direction of the canal, but since there were no mandatory lights, I decided that my lively imagination was playing tricks on me, until my sharp ears confirmed my first impression as they detected the sibilant susurration of water parted by the moving prow, and the stealthy splash of the blade wielded by the unseen gondolier as he propelled his craft up the rio.

Surely this must be some Casanova on a secret assignment, I decided, smiling to myself at the romantic notion.

I was about to turn away from the window when a light was switched on in the bedroom next to mine, and the rays streaming down from the side window suddenly illumined the patch of rio through which the gondola was moving.

I caught a brief glimpse of a girl with a long, thin, rather young face and long, pale hair, lying back against the black pillows of the boat, her eyes closed as if in anticipation of a kiss as the man by her side bent over her, almost immediately hiding her from my view.

I had an equally brief glimpse of the gondolier who propelled the craft, and who was dressed, not in the white sailor suit, crimson sash and straw hat of the picture postcard gondoliers but in what looked to me like a black rubber suit similar to the kind water skiers sometimes wear, with a black rubber cap well down on his forehead, and whether it was in contrast to the blackness of his suit, his skin seemed waxlike and his hands on the pole unusually white and slender, and the bedroom light reflected back the gleam of the broad jewelled ring he wore on his little finger as he propelled the boat out of the square of light.

Almost before it had quite disappeared from view I heard from the open window of the next room a sharp, surprised hiss, and "What the devil!" Then the distinctly American voice continued with annoyance. "Oh, damn these pesky beetles!"

There followed the sound of the window being angrily slammed shut, and of someone swatting viciously at the intruding beetles. I grinned to myself.

I had recognised the voice as belonging to the elderly woman from New York, who had monopolised the conversation at the table next to mine in the dining-room that evening. Her voice had had a sharp, nasal, carrying quality, and although I had had no intention of eavesdropping, since I had been sitting on my own it had been impossible to ignore her chatter.

Indeed, it had been her mention of sneak thieves climbing up to hotel balconies and raiding bedrooms while the occupants slept which had finally decided me which of my own bedroom windows to open only a few moments earlier.

The talkative American had certainly had a

thing about sneak thieves, even to the extent of deliberately choosing her present, smaller bedroom, with no balcony, and facing the blank wall across the rio, rather than the spacious room on the other side of mine to the front of the hotel, which was next door to that of the friends she had been with in the dining-room.

I could not help wondering what she thought of this choice now, for if my room, with its great high, wide window overlooking the open space of the lagoon felt overhot and stuffy, her one, with only one window overlooking the narrow rio, must have been even stuffier.

No doubt I would hear all about the merits of American air conditioning and American hotels at breakfast time!

I climbed back into my bed, a huge, high, almost architectural piece of furniture, which, when I had first seen it the previous evening had made me want to giggle.

Both head and foot boards were painted a deep blue, and adorned with stuccoed, intricately carved white garlands and fat, winged, baby-faced cherubs, and with its snow-white lace spread, and white muslin draperies hanging suspended overhead from its four posts, it seemed to me more suited as a bridal bed than for the resting place of a solitary spinster!

I settled down on the soft mattress, determined to snatch a few hours sleep, but bumping noises, bangs and irritated ejaculations from the next room kept me awake. I lay seeing in my mind's eye my little New York neighbour with her blue rinsed hair and enormous false eyelashes angrily chasing the pesky beetles which had invaded her privacy round and round her bedroom.

After about ten minutes the sounds of activity ceased, and I heard the click of the electric switch, a signal which seemed to proclaim that the hunter had dispatched her prey.

I sighed with relief and settled back once more against the pillows. Now, however, I was too wide awake to be able to woo sleep, so instead, I thought back to the chain of circumstances which had brought me here to Venice.

Firstly, there had been the unexpected holiday given me by my employer because he had been grateful for the amount of research and overtime I had recently done for him in connection with the project he had been working on. Secondly there had been the postcard from Ben Ferguson, showing the very view I could now see from my bedroom window, with the boldly scrawled, but meaningless message on the correspondence side of the card which said, "Wish you were here with me, Melanie!", which had given me the idea of Venice as a possible place to spend my unexpected fortnight of freedom. Finally there had been the fact that when I had gone to a travel agent I knew, and asked him about the chances of booking a holiday in Venice, he had been so enthusiastic about my proposed visit to a city which he himself loved, that before I knew what was happening, I was booked on a flight that evening from Edinburgh, and had a room reserved, by long distance call, in this hotel which he had personally recommended—and that had been that!

I stared once more out of the window towards the moonlit island of San Giorgio Maggiore, and again I was assailed by the feeling of unreality. The whole scene was too ephemeral to be true. No sound disturbed the tranquillity of the night. There was no roar of early morning traffic beneath my window as there would have been in any other great city.

I snuggled further down into the soft bed, my eyelids drooped and I relaxed into slumber to be awakened in what seemed only a few minutes but which the illuminated hands of my clock told me was over an hour later, by a muffled scream from the next room, followed by a dull thud.

I grimaced with annoyance and sat up to readjust my pillow. My American friend apparently had not been as successful as she thought she had been in getting rid of her unwanted pests, and now she was on the warpath again.

There was a succession of noises, not so loud as during the previous chase, but equally as irritating. Then there was silence for several minutes, and I was about to close my eyes once more, when this silence was shattered by a heavy bump, followed by a pained groan, and to my dismay, this eerie groaning went on and on. I tried to shut my ears to the noise, but my conscience would not let me ignore it. It was so obvious that something was wrong next door that,

like it or not, I knew I would have to find out
what had happened.

Reluctantly I crawled from my bed, pulling
my filmy negligée over my shoulders, and
without troubling to grope for my slippers which
I had inadvertently kicked under the bed a few
minutes earlier, I went out into the corridor and
knocked softly on my neighbour's door, calling
quietly as I did so.

"Is there anything wrong?"

There was no reply, but I could hear a
peculiar dragging noise, and continued painful
moaning.

I bit my lip, wondering what to do, and as I
stood there, hesitant, once again I heard that
odd, dragging sound, followed by a scrabbling on
the other side of the door, and the handle moved
slightly.

I stood waiting for the door to be opened for
me, but nothing happened, although I could
hear deep, painful breathing and a fainter moan,
and then a slithering noise and a bump, as if
whoever had tried the handle had collapsed on
the other side.

I was definitely worried now, so I turned the
handle myself and tried to push the door open.
It yielded only a few inches.

The room was in darkness, but from the light
in the corridor, I could see a clenched hand on
the floor, and the enormous diamond on the
engagement ring reflected back this light. I
shivered, and for one selfish moment I wished I
had been a heavy sleeper, so that I would not

have got myself involved in this distressing incident.

My poor neighbour must have tripped over some object in her chase after her pesky beetles, and hurt herself rather badly in the fall.

She was not even moaning now, as she had been earlier, and I guessed she must have passed out completely.

Carefully I manœuvred my way through the narrow gap, switched on the light and looked down compassionately at the slight figure crumpled up against the door.

As I looked at her, my eyes widened with horror, and without any conscious volition, I opened my mouth and uttered a piercing scream.

The very shrillness of my own scream brought me back to my senses.

Somehow I managed to bite my rising hysteria, and after a quick terrified glance round the little bedroom to assure myself that whoever had brutally plunged the leather handled dagger between the thin shoulder blades of the woman sprawled at my feet had gone, I knelt shakily down by her side, to whisper words of comfort to her before I went to summon professional help.

Only the stirring of a wisp of my honey brown hair, which brushed against the lips of her gaping mouth as I bent my head to listen for her heart beats told me she was still alive, so faint was her breathing, and with a coldness which froze the muscles round my heart, I realised that the little New Yorker was close to death, and that even the very finest medical skill would be of no avail.

Now I was torn between fear and compassion. I had never before been in contact with death, and it stirred in me some primitive terror, which urged me to flee the spot. Then the years of civilisation took control, and I knew that I could not go and leave this poor soul to die alone.

Gently I took her outstretched hand in mine and held it. At my touch, her eyes fluttered open, but there was no sight in them, only a blank, opaque stare, and I shivered as they gazed up blindly in my direction.

Then, so faintly that I could only make out a word here and there, she whispered a message to me.

It seemed she was trying to tell me about a man who had gone to leave her. Then somehow she managed to raise her head, and her eyes cleared as she murmured, "Assist and—" but the rest of her words were lost as a shrill voice from the corridor screamed.

"Henry! I told you the screeching came from Alice's room. Alice!" the voice was almost hysterical. "Are you all right?"

Someone tried to push the door further open.

"Wait, please!" I called urgently, releasing my grip of the dying woman's hand. I rose shakily to my feet and eased myself out through the narrow gap to face the hotel guests who were crowding the corridor.

I was beginning to feel cold and shivery and sick with reaction to my discovery, but I took a deep breath and managed to say:

"Please be quiet. There has been an accident. Would someone kindly fetch the manager, and call a doctor?"

My voice rose to a squeak on the last words. I tried to focus my eyes on the couple at the head of the crowd of guests. My head seemed to go cold and my scalp tingled uncomfortably. A curious feeling of being completely disembodied possessed me.

I was vaguely aware of a tall man striding to the forefront of the other chattering guests, and the excited babbling of the tall woman directly opposite me, who was the friend of the dying woman in the room behind that half-closed door, and then I felt myself falling, falling, falling into a deep pit of interminable grey, swirling fog.

Chapter Two

WHEN I recovered consciousness, I was lying on top of the bed in my own bedroom, and the man, whom I had noticed push his way towards me along the corridor, past the gaping-mouthed American couple, a few minutes earlier, was standing beside me, looking down at me with a grim expression on his face.

I tried to sit up, but he laid a detaining hand on my shoulder.

"Just lie still for another minute or two," he advised me in a deep, calm voice. "It is better not to sit up too abruptly."

Although I still felt light-headed, with returning consciousness came the memory of the scene I had witnessed in the bedroom next door, and pushing aside the man's restraining hand, I sat up, swung my legs over the edge of the bed and stood up.

"That poor woman—the elderly American—how is she?"

He looked at me sombrely.

"She is dead," he stated briefly. "There was nothing I could do for her."

I raised my hands to press them against my throbbing temples as he continued to stare down at me, the pupils of his dark hazel eyes narrowing as he asked slowly,

"In what way were you involved with this woman?"

I widened my eyes in surprise at the question.

"I didn't know her at all!" I told him. "I saw her for the first time at dinner tonight, and I did not know she occupied the room next door until—until—" I gulped back a mouthful of bile before continuing.

"I was awakened a short time ago by noises in the adjoining room. There was a bump and a cry, and after a time, a continuous moaning." I shivered. "The walls are not quite so thick as one would expect." Another tremor shook my body. "I thought the woman had got out of bed and fallen over something and hurt herself, so I went to see if I could be of any help to her."

I was shaking violently now, and the man turned from me and strode across to the old-fashioned wardrobe in the corner of the room, opened the door and pulled my light-weight travel coat from its hanger.

"Better put this on," he said brusquely. "Shock does tend to make one feel cold, even when fully clad!" His glance swept over me, making me suddenly uncomfortably conscious of the flimsiness of the negligée I was wearing, a garment which was in reality a mere wisp of white gossamer, trimmed at the off-the-shoulder neckline and scalloped hem with ribbons of white satin and which left very little to the imagination.

Blushing furiously I pulled the coat tightly

round me, and at this reaction, the man gave me an amused smile.

"Don't worry. I am used to seeing women in various types of night attire." His hazel eyes reflected the laughter in his voice. "There is no need to feel embarrassed. I am a doctor," he went on by way of explanation. "Somerville's the name. Peter Somerville."

"And I am Melanie Lindsay," I introduced myself in turn, and then went on, with a sigh of relief. "And at this moment you have no idea how glad I am that you are British too! All the Italian I know is *'Ciao'* and *'Arrivederci'*!"

"And 'No' too, I hope!" his eyes twinkled. "I gather that that is one of the most important words for a pretty girl to be able to say in Italian!"

"Or in any language!" I countered, returning his smile, and beginning to feel grateful to him for the way he was putting me at ease.

A sharp knocking on the door brought us back from our pleasantries to the hardness of reality.

"That could be the police!" The amusement faded from Somerville's face, and he eyed me keenly. "Do you think you could face up to answering their questions now, or would you rather have a little longer to pull yourself together?"

Involuntarily I pulled my coat still tighter round me, as if it was some kind of protective armour.

"I would rather see them now, and get the interview over and done with," I decided. "Do you think they will keep me very long?"

"I don't expect so," said Somerville reassuringly as he went forward to open the door. "There is not really much you can tell them, is there?"

I shook my head. "Why, no. Just about hearing the noises and the moaning and going to see what had happened."

"Well, then, there is nothing to worry about, is there?" He turned the handle of the door and opened it to admit the men who were standing outside.

I would love to have asked him if he would stay with me during the subsequent interview, but the police made it quite plain they wanted to see me on their own, and when I muttered something about not knowing any Italian, the man in charge bowed, and in excellent English told me that there would be no need for an interpreter.

I did not expect the interview to last for more than ten minutes or so, and certainly, to begin with, it seemed that all the police wanted was a straightforward account of my reasons for going to the room next door, and of my finding the dying woman.

I was not interrupted while I related my tale. The man who had come into the room along with the officer who was interrogating me made notes, and from this I gathered that he too could understand English.

When I had finished my recital there was a short silence while the officer, who had introduced himself as Captain Cerutti, consulted the notes the other man had made.

Finally he spoke. "So, Signorina Lindsay," he looked down at me, where I sat on the comfortable armchair beside the writing table. "You were asleep, you were awakened by a bump and a cry, and you immediately went to investigate?"

"Not immediately. I lay wondering what could have happened, and when the moaning started anew and went on and on, I realised my neighbour must have met with some kind of accident." I looked at him. "I felt it my duty to see if I could help her."

"I see." Cerutti took a cigarette case from his pocket and proffered it to me.

I shook my head. "I don't smoke, thank you."

He selected a cigarette for himself, lit it, inhaled a mouthful of the smoke, and then exhaled it again, in a perfect smoke ring whose progress he followed with his eyes as it drifted up towards the ceiling.

He was a slim, dapper man, and his grey uniform with its scarlet piping looked as if it had been tailor made for him. Although it was almost dawn, and he must either have been on night duty, or wakened from sleep to take over the case, he looked fresh and alert. His smooth olive cheeks were freshly shaven and he exuded an odour of expensive shaving lotion. The fingers holding the cigarette were long and smooth skinned and beautifully manicured, yet in spite of his almost dandified air, there was a steeliness in his eyes which told me this was not a man to be trifled with.

The silence continued, and I wondered why the men did not take their leave. I stifled a yawn and gazed longingly at my bed while Cerutti went on calmly smoking and glancing at the notes.

"Signorina Lindsay, tell me, what made you decide to come to Venice at this time?" Cerutti suddenly barked at me.

I looked at him in surprise.

"For a holiday, of course. What else would bring someone like me here?"

He tapped off the ash of his cigarette into the ashtray on the writing desk.

"I wonder?" he regarded me musingly for a second or two, then said:

"I understand from the manager of the hotel that your reservation was made by telephone the day before yesterday?"

"Why, yes." I frowned, wondering what his interest in this could be. "I only knew a couple of days ago that I was to be on holiday now. That was why I did not book a room until the last minute, so to speak."

"But why Venice? Why this particular hotel? Have you friends in the city?" He rapped out each question sharply, not giving me time to answer one before posing the next one.

"For goodness sake!" I exclaimed. "Why not Venice? And in any case, why this interest in my movements?"

He shrugged.

"A crime has been committed, signorina. We have to explore all the possibilities."

"You are not being serious!" I stared at him wide eyed. "Surely you don't think I had anything to do with that poor woman's death?"

"No?" he questioned.

"Don't be ridiculous!" I exclaimed angrily. "No wonder there are not so many good Samaritans in this day and age if every good deed is liable to police suspicion! I hear someone in the room next to mine moan with pain, I go to her assistance, and am accused of murder!" I stood up. "I do not in the least like your attitude, Captain Cerutti. I should like to get in touch with my Consul, here, before I say anything further!"

"Signorina!" Captain Cerutti smiled at me regretfully, "I am sorry if I have upset you, but it is my duty to probe every eventuality."

"It is your duty to go and look for the murderer of that poor woman, instead of wasting your time asking me a lot of useless questions!" I retorted. "However, if it will get you off my back more quickly, you can get in touch with my employer, who will tell you that he gave me this holiday out of the blue. You can get in touch with the travel agent who booked this holiday for me, and who chose this particular hotel himself, and not at my instigation, and I can get in touch with a friend of mine, who may still be in Venice, and tell him what I think of your police methods. I am sure he will be most interested, and might even make a story out of it. You may even know him yourself, because his name is not unknown outside his own country—Ben Ferguson, of the International Press!" I glared at him.

Whether it was my unexpected outburst, or the mention of Ben's name which did the trick,

I did not know, but one or other was effective in changing the tone of the interview.

"Signorina Lindsay!" Cerutti bowed. "I am very sorry if I have upset you. Naturally I had no intention of accusing you of being party to this dreadful affair. I was only wanting to keep my records straight."

He signalled to his man to close his notebook. "You have been of very great assistance to us, for which I must thank you. My only regret is that you could not make out all the words that the Signora Sinclair was trying to whisper to you."

Once more he eyed me keenly with those robin bright eyes of his.

"You are quite sure you have told me all that you think you heard?"

"Quite sure, Captain," I replied firmly. "I have told you everything, and I did not want to mislead you by imagining what she might have been trying to say."

"In that event, signorina, there are no further questions I wish to ask you. Should we need you at any future date, you will be at this hotel for a further fourteen days, I understand?"

I nodded.

The Captain saluted and took his leave, followed by his companion. I carefully locked the door behind them and went over to see that the windows were securely shut, although with the police swarming about the hotel it was unlikely that any other sneak thief would venture near the place that night, and then wearily took off my coat, draped it over one of the chairs, and climbed wearily into bed, where I fell asleep almost at once from sheer exhaustion.

I was awakened about three hours later by the shrill summons of the telephone on the bedside table.

I blinked rapidly against the sudden glare of daylight as I opened my eyes and, smothering a yawn, I stretched out my hand to lift the instrument off the receiver.

"Melanie," said a well-remembered voice. "What is all this I hear about your coming to Venice to start a crime wave?"

"Ben!" I gasped, and sat up in bed with a jerk. "You are still in Venice! How wonderful! I was so sure you would be away somewhere else by this time!" I almost choked with relief and happiness.

"Oh, Ben! You simply can have no idea how wonderful it is to know that you are at hand at this moment!"

Ben chuckled. "I rather gathered from my friend Captain Cerutti that you were in need of someone to keep an eye on you!"

"Ben, where are you? How soon can I see you?" I demanded impatiently.

"I am 'phoning from the reception desk downstairs, Melanie, and how soon you can see me depends on yourself. I was actually hoping we might breakfast together?"

"Oh! I am still in bed, Ben, but give me five minutes to get dressed, and I shall be delighted to breakfast with you!" I exclaimed joyfully.

"I shall be waiting for you in the foyer, Melanie," he replied, and replaced the receiver.

Chapter Three

I SHIVERED with excitement as I jumped from the bed. Although the postcard I had received from Ben Ferguson had been partly instrumental in my choice of Venice as a holiday spot, I had not for a single moment expected that he would still be there when I arrived.

Ben never seems to be in any one place for more than a few days. His job takes him to all the trouble spots of the world and I was as liable to get a postcard from him from Vancouver as from Venice.

Ben is ten years older than I am, and I have known him for the past seven years, since I was fourteen, when his parents retired to live in the cottage next door to the manse where I had been born and brought up.

I had been an enthusiastic stamp collector in those days and when I learned that the god-like being of twenty-four who occasionally appeared to spend a weekend with his parents had a job which took him all over the globe, I had plucked up courage to ask him to get me a few stamps from the various places he visited.

Ben had not only sent me innumerable stamps, but also postcards from the places he went to, and the drawer of my desk at home overflowed with pictures of all sorts of romantic spots, from Tokyo to Turkestan and Paris to Peru.

As I grew older, I fancied myself in love with the gay, laughing-eyed young man next door, although I doubt if he really noticed I was growing up, for he treated me as he had always done, with an affectionate brotherliness, as if I was still a young and tongue-tied schoolgirl instead of the smart, sophisticated young woman with a responsible job, which I now was.

Perhaps, away from the atmosphere of home, in the romantic surroundings of Venice, he might view me differently I thought optimistically, as I pulled open the wardrobe door and tried to make the difficult decision as to what to wear to make the most impact on the man who still attracted me so much.

It was nearer fifteen minutes than five when I eventually met Ben in the foyer, but from the surprised and admiring look in his eyes as he came forward to give me a warm greeting, I felt that the extra trouble I had taken over my choice of dress, a simple, gorse gold linen suit which emphasised the golden lights of my corn coloured hair and the gold glints in my greenish eyes, had been worth the effort.

"How is my favourite girl friend?" he smiled at me, taking my hand in his firm, strong grip. "You certainly do not look as if you had spent a troubled night. In fact, Melanie," he went on, eyeing me appreciatively, "I had forgotten what a pretty girl you are!"

"And I had forgotten what a handsome, distinguished-looking man you are!" I rejoined, smiling up at him as I withdrew my hand from his clasp.

Ben laughed and, taking me by the elbow, guided me towards the breakfast room.

I had been so excited about the prospect of seeing Ben again, I had almost forgotten the tragedy of the previous night, but now, as I walked into the room, the other diners, several of whom had come crowding into the corridor outside of Alice Sinclair's room last night in answer to my terrified scream, turned to look at me with undisguised interest, and I felt acutely self conscious.

Ben gave my elbow a reassuring squeeze, and I continued on my way, glancing quickly from table to table to see if I could spot the young doctor who had been so kind and helpful to me after my collapse.

When I noticed him sitting alone at a table for two at the window, and staring out across the lagoon, I felt I should go over and thank him for what he had done for me, yet at the same time I was reluctant to do so in front of all those staring eyes.

The table to which the head waiter was leading us was in the window embrasure next to the one where Peter Somerville was sitting, and as I approached it I turned to Ben and said: "You have not told me why you are still here in Venice, Ben. What is keeping you in the city? Work, or one of your pretty blondes?"

Ben smiled down at me. "You know perfectly

well that you are the only woman in my life, Melanie!" he retorted gaily.

Ben has a very clear, carrying voice, and when he spoke my name, I heard a movement at the table we were passing, and Dr. Somerville pushed back his chair, stood up, and addressed me.

"Good morning, Miss Lindsay." His dark grey eyes regarded me intently. "You do not look any the worse for the shock you had last night. But how do you feel?"

"Oh! Good morning, Dr. Somerville!" I stopped beside him. "I feel much more myself now, and contrary to my expectations, I slept like a log. The pill you left for me to swallow proved most effective. Thank you so much!" I smiled at him.

As I was speaking, I was aware of Ben's surprised look from me to the other man, and also of the slight frown on Somerville's face as he glanced at Ben, and the proprietorial way Ben was still holding on to my elbow.

"Ben," I turned to him, "this is Dr. Somerville, who came to my assistance last night when I collapsed after my gruesome discovery in the room next to mine." I shivered. "You have no idea how good and kind he was to me. Dr. Somerville," I looked in turn at my new acquaintance, "this is Ben Ferguson, an old family friend, who, fortunately for me in the circumstances, happens to be in Venice on business at the moment."

The two men shook hands, acknowledging the introduction, but the doctor's eyes had lost the

friendly look they had held when he had first
addressed me, and I detected a coolness in his
voice as he replied.

"What a fortunate coincidence for you, Miss
Lindsay, to run across an old friend in Venice at
such a time."

"Yes, isn't it?" rejoined Ben cheerfully, giving
my arm an affectionate squeeze. "I am going to
make sure that Melanie does not get into any
more trouble during the rest of her stay here!"

He gently nudged me forward towards our
own table, where the waiter was standing with a
chair drawn out for me to take my place.

I was seated with my back to Somerville's
table, but as we ate our breakfast, I noticed that
Ben kept looking towards the other man, with a
faint frown on his face.

"Don't you like the look of my helpful doctor?" I queried jokingly. "From the expression
on your face, I would say you did not approve of
him!"

Ben shook his head thoughtfully. "He puzzles
me. When you introduced us I had a feeling that
I had seen him somewhere before, but I just
can't place him."

"I know one thing," I teased. "If I had met
someone like Peter Somerville before, I wouldn't
have forgotten. He is quite a dish!"

I expected Ben to make a joking reply, but to
my surprise he ignored my remark, and spoke as
if he had not even heard it.

"I don't like it when my memory plays me
tricks like this." He bit his lower lip thoughtfully. "I remember the face quite clearly, and

the name, but what was it in connection with?" His frown deepened as he glanced once more across my shoulder at the man we had been discussing.

"You don't know where he comes from, by any chance, do you?"

"Really, Ben!" I was half amused, half annoyed at Ben's preoccupation with the doctor. "I only met Somerville for a few brief moments last night, and our meeting was not a social occasion, I can assure you of that! In the circumstances, we simply did not think of exchanging life histories!" I concluded ironically.

Ben was only half listening to me. "It's odd, but somehow I don't associate him with medicine. Are you sure he is a doctor?"

"That is what he told me, and there was no reason for him to lie, was there?" I demanded tartly.

"I think I shall have a discreet look at the hotel register and see what I can learn from it," decided Ben.

"Oh, Ben!" I expostulated. "Don't you ever get tired of prying into other people's lives?"

"It is part of my job to be interested in other people," he replied. "I am a newsman, remember, and people are what make news."

"Is that why you came to see me so promptly this morning?" I demanded sharply. "Because I have news value, and not because I was a friend in need?"

"Shall we say a bit of both?" replied Ben imperturbably. "I heard a young woman was involved in an incident which will make today's news headlines, so the newspaper man in me urged me to come and talk to you." His eyes twinkled at my look of indignation as he went on.

"As it happens, as well as being newsworthy, you are also my favourite girl-next-door, which was why I asked you to breakfast with me, and why I am also hoping to persuade you to join me for dinner tonight at Harry's Bar. How about it?"

He crumpled his napkin and placed it on the plate in front of him as he posed the question.

"Harry's Bar!" I echoed. "Harry's Bar!" I repeated, my mouth stretching to a grin. "That is a date!" I confirmed before he could change his mind. "Harry's Bar is one of those places I have heard so much about I was determined to visit it, even if it was not the done thing for a young female on her own to do so!"

I poured myself a fresh cup of coffee.

"Hemingway used to go there, didn't he?"

Ben nodded. "And Orson Wells, and most of the notables who come to Venice from time to time, including me!" he added modestly.

I laughed. Ben is always fun to be with, and Venice, with Ben to take me around, was going to be even more wonderful a holiday than I had ever expected it to be. I looked at him questioningly, as I posed the question which had arisen in my mind.

"How much longer are you going to be in Venice, Ben?"

He took a packet of cigarettes from his

pocket, extracted one and lit it before he made his answer.

"That depends how things go." He inhaled a mouthful of smoke. "The Alice Sinclair affair is merely a news bonus as far as I am concerned. I am here because Martin Radcliffe and his daughter are staying in Venice at the moment."

"Martin Radcliffe, the American financier?" I queried.

Ben nodded. "He is supposed to be here on holiday, and to all intents and purposes he and his girl, who is a very pretty blonde, by the way," he added teasingly, "are doing all the things tourists customarily do in Venice—visiting the Accademia and San Marco and the Doge's Palace, shopping in the Merceria, bathing at the Lido, and dining at the Taverna La Fenice or Harry's Bar. For that matter we may see them there this evening. But I have a hunch that this visit is to cover that fact that he has come to Italy to talk about a merger with his Italian counterpart in the chemical field, and a merger between two such firms is big news. Very big news."

"I hope he doesn't make up his mind to merge for a fortnight, then!" I said lightly. "I understand that one needs a good guide to appreciate Venice, and I was hoping you might play the part for me on some occasions?"

"From the way he keeps looking across at you, I think your doctor friend would not mind understudying for me on occasion!" said Ben. "I think you have made a conquest there!"

"Don't be silly!" I shook my head. "He simply

cannot help looking at me, the way his chair is facing."

Ben's eyes narrowed. "No. I would say he is definitely interested. All the same," he shook his head, "I don't think I shall give my blessing to a holiday romance with him until I remember where it was I saw him. This loss of memory is damnably irritating," he concluded with a note of exasperation in his voice.

"You are getting old, Ben!" I teased him. "What with planning holiday romances and losing your memory, I can see you settling for a nine to five office job back home any day at all now!"

We were about to rise and leave the table when Captain Cerutti, the police officer who had interrogated me the previous night, entered the dining-room, and strode across to join us.

"Good morning Signor Ferguson, Signorina Lindsay," he bowed to us in greeting. "May I join you?"

"We were just about to leave," replied Ben cautiously. "Was there something you wanted specially to see us about?"

Cerutti pulled up a vacant chair from a nearby table.

"Yes," he said crisply. "I was hoping to get in touch with you, Signorina Lindsay, before you left the hotel this morning." His bright eyes looked at me piercingly.

"Yes?" I queried. "How can I help you?"

"I have read over the statement you gave me last night several times, signorina," he said slowly, "and each time I am puzzled, not so much by what you have said, as by what you appear not to have said in your statement."

"I don't understand." I frowned. "I told you everything I thought relevant."

"So?" he shrugged. "Then you confirm that you had never met the Signora Sinclair previously?"

"Of course!" I exclaimed sharply.

"Then how is it, signorina, that you knew who was sleeping in the room next to yours, if you had not met her before you entered the room where the crime was committed?" There was no friendliness in my questioner's voice as he rapped out the query.

"Oh!" I exclaimed. "I never thought of that! Of course that must have struck you as odd!" I gave a nervous laugh.

Ben looked at me with a frown.

"Melanie! What have you been up to? Don't you realise how serious a case this is? One doesn't hide facts in a murder investigation, however irrelevant you may think them."

Our voices had risen appreciably during the conversation, and what we were saying was obviously attracting the attention of the guests at the tables nearby.

"I wasn't trying to hide anything," I said with a shake of the head, "I was telling you the truth when I said that I had never met the American woman before. You see," I took a deep breath before I started the involved explanation, "it was like this. I think I told you that I had seen Mrs. Sinclair and her friends in the dining-room yesterday evening?"

Captain Cerutti nodded.

"They were seated at the table next to mine, and I could hear them talk. Mrs. Sinclair had a distinctive way of speaking, with a very clear, carrying, strong Yankee accent. I remember thinking at the time I would know her anywhere again by her voice alone." I paused.

"Anyway, to get on with the story, during the night, I found it impossible to get to sleep because of the heat, and eventually, it must have been about two o'clock, I got up to open the side window in my room to let in some cooler air. Mrs. Sinclair must have had the same idea, because when I was standing at my window, incidentally I had not switched on my own light for fear of attracting mosquitoes, a light suddenly appeared from the window next door. I could see it shine across the little canal and reflect back from the blank wall opposite. Then I heard the window being opened, and then," I half smiled at the memory, "I heard a loud hiss of surprise, and a voice exclaimed most clearly, 'Damn those pesky beetles!' and then the window was slammed shut. I recognised the voice as being that of Mrs. Sinclair, and then I heard her move about her room, making swiping noises as if she was chasing her pesky beetles all over the place, and a number of very choice exclamations when she missed!"

"Ah!" Cerutti nodded. "So that explains how you knew who was next door! But now, tell me, are you quite sure you heard her close the window after the beetles flew in?"

I thought back to the moment.

"Yes, I am fairly sure that I heard her slam it shut, but I can't remember if I heard her shoot the bolt back into position." I looked at him. "Do you think her assailant came in by the window?"

"We were puzzled about that. Her sister had been so insistent about how careful Mrs. Sinclair was about bolting windows and doors, that we could not understand how he entered her room, unless she had opened the door to him herself, which seemed very unlikely. However, what you have told us helps to explain what must have happened."

He stood up. "If anything else comes to your mind about last night, however trivial and unconnected with the event it may seem, will you get in touch with me, please, signorina? We have so very little to go on—" he sighed.

Before I could reply, a waiter came hurrying towards us to tell the police captain that he was wanted on the telephone. Cerutti took his leave of us, and a few seconds later we followed him from the breakfast room.

Peter Somerville was standing talking to a pretty blonde near the reception desk as we passed, and Ben shot him another puzzled glance.

"I must find out where it was I saw your doctor friend before," he muttered, more to himself than to me.

"You are like a dog with a bone!" I teased him. "Once you get your teeth into something you don't like to let go!"

"Bulldog Ferguson, that's me!" He turned to me with a smile, then glanced at his watch.

"I hadn't realised how late it is. Sorry, Melanie, but I shall have to leave you now. However, I shall call for you tonight at seven-thirty. Will that suit you?"

I nodded.

"Don't get into any more scrapes before then!" he adjured me, giving me a brief touch on the shoulder.

"*Ciao* for now!"

Chapter Four

BEN TOOK his leave, and because I did not want to follow him immediately out of the hotel, I went across to the stand beside the reception desk and selected some postcards to send to my friends back home.

I had just paid for them, when the reporters who had been hanging around the foyer realised who I was, no doubt given the tip by the hall porter who had been speaking to one of them.

In an instant I was surrounded by newsmen asking me questions, jostling to get near to me to hear more than their colleagues, or instructing me to stand still so that their photographers could take my picture for the afternoon editions.

"Look, I have told the police all I know. I have nothing to add to my original story," I said to them.

"Is it true that Mrs. Sinclair described her assailant to you before she died?" asked one.

"Of course she didn't!" I replied angrily.

"But she did say something, didn't she?" he persisted hopefully.

"I told the police what I thought she said. If they want to release the report, well and good, but I have been warned to say nothing." I spoke firmly. "Now, if you will please let me pass, I wish to go to my room."

"One more picture, signorina. Look this way, please!" I blinked in the brilliance of the flash light and looked imploringly towards the hotel manager who had appeared on the scene.

He signalled to two policemen who had been stolidly watching the proceedings from the foot of the stairs, and at his request, they ordered the men to leave the hotel. Those who showed any reluctance to do so were firmly pushed towards the door, in spite of their noisy protests.

I hastily retired to my room, where I sat for a time writing postcards, and reading the little guide book of Venice which I had brought with me.

The sunlight was beginning to flood into the room, and I looked out and thought what a waste of a lovely day it would be if I had to spend it skulking up here to escape from the newshounds. I went out onto the balcony and peered down at the Riva below. To my relief, there seemed to be no cameramen or reporters hanging around the entrance of the hotel, and after a brief hesitation, I decided it must now be safe for me to venture out without attracting unwanted attention.

When I descended to the foyer, the manager was standing talking to the Lawrences, but when he saw me, he came forward to apologise to me for any inconvenience I had been caused, and to assure me that the police had had a word with the men outside, and warned them to leave me alone.

"Not that they need to be warned off," he added. "It seems that there was a strong rumour of some other story about to break and, like vultures, they have gone to hunt for their new victim." He shrugged. "I am sure they will trouble you no more."

I bought some stamps at the desk, and posted my mail, and then as I was about to leave the hotel, the manager came hurrying after me to hand me a little booklet, the Carnet di Venezia, which, he told me, I would find most helpful, since it gave the times and tariffs and landing stages of the gondolas and other water buses on the lagoon and canals.

I thanked him and put it into my handbag, and moved uneasily towards the door, still fearing that there might be a reporter or two lurking there to accost me, but as I stepped out into the bright sunlight, no one paid the slightest attention.

A new story had broken. Already Alice Sinclair's murder was yesterday's news, as far as the press was concerned.

Although it was only mid-May, and the tourist season was not yet in full swing, the Riva degli Schiavonni was quite crowded. I stood for a moment or two watching the masses move past, and listening to the babel of tongues. Tall blondes from Sweden strode purposefully past, stout little French husbands pompously explained some point to their wives with a flurry of gesticulating hands, graceful Indian women in colourful saris glided behind their husbands in neat western suits—

Venice, it seemed, was a tourist melting pot of nations.

I followed the general drift of the crowd along the Mole towards the Piazzetta and then moved towards the water's edge to admire the view.

Across the stretch of the lagoon, the island of San Giorgio Maggiore, which had seemed so ephemeral last night in the moonlight, seemed every bit as insubstantial in the shimmering Venetian daylight.

In comparison, the great white-painted liner which lay in the channel to my right and the two sombre grey warships near the Dogano, had a solid, earthbound quality, yet seemed entirely out of place.

I decided that the contrast would make an excellent photograph, then remembered to my annoyance that I had left my camera in my bedroom.

It seemed senseless to wander about on a sightseeing tour without it, so I turned round abruptly to return to the hotel to fetch it and, as I did so, I inadvertently trod on the toe of a little man who must have been standing very close behind me.

I hadn't been aware of his presence, and I let out such a startled exclamation as I bumped into him that several passers-by looked round to see what was happening.

I flushed with embarrassment and tried to remember enough Italian to apologise to the poor man, who must have suffered agonies with the full weight of my foot on his polished shoe cap, but before I could even frame the first word of apology, without even looking at me he went hurrying off and disappeared in the throng of tourists.

I started to smile. Perhaps he was afraid that the passers-by would think he had tried to make a pass at me and did not want to have attention drawn to himself by waiting for my apology!

I was still smiling at the thought as I went up to my room to fetch my camera.

I spent the next hour happily taking snaps of the views that interested me, from the gondolas tossing at their moorings to angled shots of the characteristic Venetian lamp lights, and a study of a newsvendor at the corner of the Piazzetta.

By the time I had reached St. Mark's Square, there was only one shot left in the camera, and so I finished the reel by taking the usual scene of people feeding the plump pigeons, and went to sit at a café table on the edge of the square, where I could sip coffee, and watch the people pass by.

As I raised my hand to beckon a waiter, from the corner of my eyes I saw a little man seat himself at one of the tables not far from mine.

I frowned. This was the same man whose foot I had trodden on about an hour ago, and whom I had fancied once or twice, when I had stopped to take photographs, I had seen loitering not far from me.

I knew I was not mistaken about this, because although on the whole he was quite an ordinary looking individual, and in fact could even be described as quite inconspicuous looking, two things about him had attracted my attention at what could be called our first meeting—the size of his feet, which were unusually big for such a little man, and the highly-polished and very pointed shoes which he wore, and which I could not have helped noticing at that first encounter!

Was it purely coincidence that he had chosen this very café to come to at this very moment, or had our chance meeting interested him in me? He did not look the Casanova type, but he might have seen himself in that light and, realising that I was on my own, thought he might have a chance of furthering our acquaintanceship.

I decided to pretend not to notice him, since any show of interest on my part might be taken as an invitation. All the same, I did not feel too happy sitting there on my own, and if the waiter had not come at that moment for my order, I might have moved away.

I glanced ostentatiously at my watch, hoping that this would indicate that I was waiting for someone, but the gesture did not really help me. All that it did was to tell me that it was nearly ten-thirty, and that it would be nine hours before I would see Ben again.

Now the day in which I had planned to do so much seemed to stretch interminably before me. Damn the little man, I thought angrily. Why should I let him annoy me? If he was silly enough to make any advances, I would tell him where he got off in no uncertain manner, even if my command of Italian was none too good, a brush off is a brush off in any language!

Having made this resolution, I moved my

chair, so that I sat with my back to him, took off my sunglasses and gazed admiringly across the Square at the façade of San Marco. The front of the great cathedral was in shadow, but this shadow was not deep enough to dim the beauty of the five porches, and the magnificent mosaics, which I intended to examine and admire at my leisure later on.

Although the face of the cathedral was in shadow, the morning sun illumined the many domes of the Basilica, and brushed the eagles atop the flagpoles with pure gold. This same sun, shining behind the great Campanile which towered above the Square, made it cast a deep, deep shadow and traverse the well-worn flags of the Piazza, where the pigeons were as yet more numerous than the tourists who crowded to feed them.

I turned round to order a second cup of coffee, and noticed with annoyance that my pointed-shoed admirer had moved to the table next to mine. He wasn't looking at me, but I had the feeling that he had been doing so, and had only switched his glance away when I had turned to summon the waiter.

The elderly waiter, with a badge bearing his number, returned to take my order, and when he had gone, a couple of hawkers who had been lingering on the pavement nearby, came up to me to try to persuade me to buy their wares. I firmly refused to buy anything from the postcard seller, and the old woman with a tray load of cheap souvenirs, but my gasp of delight when I looked at the huge basket filled with carnations of every possible hue, and bunches of other lovely blooms which a stout flower seller in a drab black dress, but with a bright, smiling face, thrust almost under my nose, seemed to convince her that she would be able to persuade me to buy some of her fragrant blossoms.

I tried to explain to her that although I thought the flowers were lovely, there wasn't much use in buying them, as I was living in a hotel, but she pretended not to understand that "No" means "No" in Italian as well as in English, and proceeded to make up a multi-coloured bouquet which she tried to thrust into my hand.

"No, please. No!" I shook my head. "I do not want them! *Mon li voglio!*" I stammered out the Italian phrase, but still she held them out to me.

I looked hopefully towards the waiter who was bringing me my coffee, hoping that he would set the woman about her business, but before he reached my table, a voice in English said from behind me: "You seem to be having some trouble, Miss Lindsay. Can I be of help?"

I looked round gratefully to see Peter Somerville standing smiling down at me.

"I don't seem able to make her understand that I don't want to buy her flowers." I shook my head. "My Italian isn't very good, and I made the mistake of admiring the flowers in the first place. They are gorgeous, aren't they?"

"I like the camellias," he said, bending down, and selecting a bunch from the flower seller's basket. "They don't flaunt themselves quite so brazenly as the carnations, do they?"

He handed some silver coins to the woman, who beamed at him, and muttered *"Grazie"* at least a dozen times before taking herself off.

Somerville placed the flowers on the table beside me. "That was the coward's way out, I suppose, but I think it was the quickest way to get rid of her, don't you?" He smiled at me. "Now, since I can hardly wander round Venice carrying a bunch of camellias, will you accept them from me?"

"They are lovely!" I beamed with delight. "Thank you very much!"

I looked down at the flowers, and gently touched the waxen petals with my fingertip. "They are so perfect, they hardly seem real."

"That is how I think I would describe Venice herself," observed Dr. Somerville, glancing all about him. "This is my first visit here, and the more I see of the city, the more fascinated I am. I cannot understand how Montaigne could have found it less wonderful than he had imagined, can you?"

I shook my head. "It surpasses all that I had imagined and that is saying something!"

Peter Somerville hesitated.

"Are you waiting for your friend, or may I join you for coffee?" he asked.

"I am on my own," I told him, "and I should be delighted if you would join me. Your presence should surely discourage the attentions of a little man who seems to be taking too much interest in me for comfort!"

"What man is that?" demanded Somerville in a belligerent tone, looking round him.

"The one at the table right behind me," I said.

Somerville grinned. "I must have done my discouraging act already! That table is now vacant."

I looked quickly round and sighed with relief.

"Thank goodness for that. He was beginning to get on my nerves! It isn't really much fun to be on one's own at times like that!"

Somerville sat down at the table. "I don't suppose it is," he agreed. "I expect you will be glad that Ferguson is in Venice to keep you company."

"I don't expect that I shall be seeing very much of Ben," I said. "He is not in Venice on holiday, you know. He is a journalist, and is just waiting for some story he is working on to break, and then he will be moving on somewhere else. That could mean tomorrow, or the next day, he will pack his bags and be off."

"So meeting him really was a coincidence?" Somerville said cheerfully.

"A very pleasant one, I must admit. Ben and I are very good friends, and I am rather hoping his story won't break for a few more days, so that I can persuade him to show me some of the Venetian highlights."

The doctor signalled to the waiter and ordered a coffee.

"I am in Venice partly on pleasure and partly on duty," he informed me. "As it happens, I shall be free this afternoon, and since it is such a lovely day I had been thinking of going across to the Lido for a bathe." He gave me a quizzical look. "If you have nothing else planned, would you like to join me?"

"I hadn't yet decided what I was going to do later today," I said slowly.

"Which means you are free to accept my invitation?" he asked hopefully.

I hesitated.

There was no reason why I should not spend the afternoon with Peter Somerville. He was an extremely attractive man. I had found him friendly and kindly the previous evening, when I had been in need of friendliness and kindliness, and if Ben had not expressed some doubt about him, I would have accepted the invitation straightaway.

But Ben must be mistaken about him, I thought, looking at the man from under my long eyelashes. I had liked what I had seen of him at our first encounter. I liked his manner and I liked his looks and I decided to stick to my first impression of him.

"I should very much like to go with you to the Lido," I assured him. "I want to acquire a good sun tan before I go home, or my friends won't believe I have been abroad, and I can hardly acquire a tan if I spend all my time in museums and art galleries, can I?"

"Hardly!" he agreed.

We exchanged a few pleasantries, and then Somerville told me he would have to keep an appointment he had made earlier that morning. I wondered with an odd twinge if he had a luncheon date with the pretty girl I had seen him talking to after breakfast, but at least, I cheered myself, he is not going swimming with her this afternoon!

We agreed to meet at our hotel at two o'clock, and Peter went off for his luncheon appointment, while I picked up my bouquet of camellias and retraced my steps to the hotel on the Riva degli Schiavonni, happily unaware that as I bade farewell to the young doctor, the little man with the pointed shoes, who had been watching us from behind one of the pillars in the arcade across the Square, was preparing to dog my footsteps once again.

Chapter Five

I HAD originally intended to lunch at Quadri's in St. Mark's Square, but the unexpected gift of flowers from Peter Somerville had changed my mind about this. If my lovely camellias were not put into a vase of water within the hour, they would be brown and wilted, and since I did not want this to happen, I decided to return straightaway to my hotel and ask the chambermaid for a container for them.

Thereafter, since I had arranged to meet Peter at two o'clock in the foyer, it would be more sensible to dine in the hotel restaurant than to go out again.

It was now after twelve o'clock, and with the sun at its height, I felt uncomfortably warm in my tailored linen suit as I walked across the Piazzetta to the shaded arcade of the Doges Palace.

My progress was slower than I had anticipated. I seemed to be fighting against a tide of humanity which was surging up towards St. Mark's Square, everyone intent, no doubt, as I had been earlier, of finding a table at Quandri's or Florian's or one of the other famous restaurants which line the Piazza.

In the crush I found it difficult to cope with

my camera, flowers and bulky shoulder bag into
which I had crammed my guidebook, the map of
Venice which I had been told was necessary if I
did not want to lose my way in the city when I
went sightseeing, my book of traveller's cheques,
and a small jewel case which contained the few
good pieces of jewellery which I had brought
with me and which, after last night, I felt might
be safer in my possession than left in a drawer in
the hotel bedroom.

At the angle of the Doge's Palace, where the
Piazzetta joins the Mole, I stopped beside one of
the souvenir stalls, away from the crowds, laid
my bunch of flowers on the counter to give me a
free hand, and with a bit of a struggle, managed
to cram my camera in with all the other things
which were in my shoulder bag.

The young stall-holder who had approached
me when he saw me open my bag, gave a disgruntled exclamation when I picked up my
flowers again and prepared to move off, and tried
to detain me by offering one of his ornately
carved gondola models at bargain price, but I ignored his persuasive voice and pleading eyes,
and slinging my bag back over my shoulder, continued on my way down the Mole.

At the bottleneck of the Ponte della Paglia
which leads from the Mole to the Riva degli
Schiavonni, the jostling of the crowd seemed to
reach its peak, and I found myself brought
almost to a standstill by the crush of bodies.

I felt quite breathless with the pushing and
shoving and I was afraid that my lovely little

bouquet would be crushed to pieces before I reached my destination.

Up until now I had been keeping a firm grip of my shoulder bag with my right hand, since crowds are where the bag snatchers operate in any city, but now I was more concerned at the probable mutilation of the camellias than the possibility of having my bag stolen, so I slung the bag behind my back and used both hands to protect my precious bouquet as I pushed my way forward, through a fresh crowd of people who had newly disembarked from the vaporetto at the nearby landing stage.

One large, aggressive-looking woman in the centre of the pack strode determinedly forward, steering a collision course in my direction. Realising that I would be the one to come off worst in the encounter, I hastily side-stepped to escape being mown down.

At the very instant that I made the sideways manœuvre I felt a strong tug at my shoulder bag, as if someone behind me was making a grab at it.

I whirled round angrily, and was just in time to see the little man I had noticed so often earlier in the day pushing his way back into the crowd, where he was almost immediately lost to view. I made to follow him, and as I did so, my bag started to slither to the ground. I stopped and grabbed at it, and to my indignation, found that the strap which had been attached to it had been severed by the knife which was still embedded in the leather side of the bag.

I stopped in my tracks, literally winded with

the fury of indignation which seized me. The man with the pointed shoes whom I had dismissed as a would-be Casanova had been a hopeful sneak thief who had marked me down as his victim!

No doubt he had seen me come out of the hotel on my own that morning, and both because I was on my own and because I was staying at a first-class hotel and wore clothes which his practised eye would assess as being of good quality, he had decided that I would be worthy of his attentions.

People surged uncaring round me as I continued to stand glaring at the spot where he had disappeared into the crowd, clutching my mutilated bag with one hand, and somehow still holding onto my camellias which by some miracle were still intact.

I was so angry I could have screamed aloud, but somehow I pulled myself together and went striding back to the hotel, bumping uncaringly against whoever got in my way. Venice, I thought angrily, might be one of the world's most beautiful cities, but it seemed to me that it had more than its fair share of thieves!

Captain Cerutti had told me that Mrs. Sinclair's room had been ransacked after she had been attacked, and all her money and jewellery except the rings she wore on her wedding finger had been taken, and his theory was that the poor woman had wakened up and disturbed the thief at work, and been killed by him in a panic to prevent her crying out.

It was not pleasant to think that a thief could

be panicked into murder, particularly when I thought how easily the same thing could have happened to me just now if I had whirled round a second sooner and caught the thief in his act. As it was, he probably felt quite sure that I had not spotted him. I sincerely hoped that he would continue to think so!

Nervous perspiration damped my clothes at my frightening thoughts, and I glanced with distaste at the haft of the knife which was still wedged into the bag I was carrying.

Not many people would have such a holiday souvenir to take home with them, I thought with grim humour.

I stepped from the bright sunlight of the Riva into what at first seemed the darkness of the hotel hall, and had to stand for a few seconds to let my eyes accustom themselves to the change of light.

When I moved into the foyer, the first people I saw were Captain Cerutti and the other smart young officer who had been with him when he had interviewed me the night before.

They were standing beside the gilded case in the centre of the hall, which served as the hotel lift, talking to the manager.

The two policemen had their backs to me, which was just as well for me, for when I had first noticed them, I had taken an involuntary step forward, to tell them with justifiable indignation, of what had happened to me a few moments earlier, but no sooner had I taken a couple of steps in their direction than I changed my mind.

What good would complaining to the police do? Apart from my ruined shoulder bag, which I should be able to replace fairly cheaply in Venice, no harm had been done. On the other hand, if I poured out my tale to Captain Cerutti, I was bound to get involved in a fresh police inquiry, and I had had enough of police inquisitions last night to last me a lifetime.

Instead, therefore, of approaching Cerutti, I veered towards the desk to collect the key for my room.

I was heading for the stairs when Captain Cerutti called after me.

"Ah! Signorina Lindsay!"

I stopped with one foot on the lowest step of the stairway, and turned reluctantly round to see Cerutti and his handsome aide striding towards me.

I hurriedly moved my bunch of flowers to cover completely the knife which I had left embedded in the side of my bag.

"Yes?" I asked, my eyes narrowing warily in case I was going to be detained for more questions about the affair of the previous night.

As if aware of what I was thinking, Cerutti shook his head, smiling.

"It is all right, signorina. My present business with you is not official." His eyes strayed to the flowers I was carrying, and for a moment his eyes held a puzzled look.

"The Signor Ferguson asked me to leave a message here for you when he learned that I was returning to the Hotel Capri. I was delivering it to the manager, when he noticed your return, so I have come to deliver it in person."

"Don't tell me that Signor Ferguson is going to call off our date at Harry's Bar this evening!" I groaned.

Cerutti shook his head and smiled reassuringly.

"No, no! He will keep his appointment, but he wanted to let you know that he might be a little later than arranged." His eyes kept glancing at the bouquet I was gripping, so that I was sure that he must have spotted the knife which I was trying to hide, and I felt myself tense nervously as I wondered how I could explain its presence without actually saying what had happened.

However, Cerutti's next words were merely an explanation of why Ben would not be able to come for me at the appointed time.

"You see," he went on to explain, "Signor Ferguson has had to go to Padua on business, and he is not sure how long he will be detained there."

"Oh!" I exclaimed. "I should have known better than arrange a date with him! This is invariably what happens. His news stories come before his social obligations!"

The police captain shrugged.

"In some professions, signorina, it is very difficult to arrange a social life. My wife also complains about the hours I keep and the amount of food she ruins when I do not come home on time for a meal. I explained that this is how it would be before we were married, as I dare say Signor Ferguson has explained to you."

"I am not going to marry Signor Ferguson!" I blushed with embarrassment. "He is an old friend of the family, that is all!"

Cerutti's eyebrows shot up in ill-concealed disbelief. "So?" he shrugged, and once again his eyes strayed to the camellias. "Allora, I have delivered my message, signorina, and now I must be on my way." He gave a polite little bow.

"Arrivederci!"

I echoed the word as he turned on his elegant heels, and his equally elegant *tenente* saluted and followed him across the hall and out of the building.

I hurried upstairs to my room and rang for the chambermaid to bring me a vase for my flowers.

While I waited for her to come, I gingerly pulled the knife out of my bag and examined the damage it had done. My camera case inside the bag was also badly scored, as if it had taken much of the force of the blow, but apart from a slight dent, the camera itself was not harmed.

I put the dagger, a leather-hafted weapon with an exceptionally sharp blade, although its point was now blunted from the impact, into the envelope which had contained the postcards I had bought that morning, and popped it into one of my empty travel cases.

Further inspection of my bag made me decide that it would not be worth repairing, and I was about to drop it into the waste paper basket when there was a knock at the door to announce the arrival of the chambermaid.

I was still holding onto the bag when I opened

the door to her, and her quick expressive eyes immediately noticed the ragged gash in it.

She murmured something in rapid Italian, but I could not understand what she was saying. She spoke again, more slowly, and I gathered that she was telling me of someone she knew who would repair the bag for me.

I shook my head. As far as I was concerned, the bag would never be the same again, and I would rather buy a new one, so I asked her if the repair shop also sold bags.

"*Si*," she nodded, but I could tell from the expression on her face that she thought I was mad to waste money on a new bag when the old one could be cheaply mended.

With a shake of her head at my extravagance, she went to the bathroom to fill the pretty blue Murano glass vase she was carrying with water from the bath tap.

When she returned to arrange the flowers for me, I asked her if she would like to keep the bag.

A volley of *grazies* and a delighted smile greeted this offer, and a few minutes later she left the bedroom clutching her prize tightly to her bosom, almost as if she was afraid I would have a last-minute change of mind.

I re-arranged the camellias and carried the vase over to the bedside table. I sat down on the bed and looked at them with pleasure, thinking of the romantic story I would be able to tell when I returned home, about how I had been presented with a lovely bouquet of flowers by a tall, dark and handsome stranger on my very first day in Venice!

Not that I thought of Peter Somerville as a stranger. Somehow I felt that we must have met somewhere before, because I felt so relaxed in his presence, but perhaps this was merely because he had such a pleasant manner he immediately put one at one's ease.

I could imagine that he would be a popular doctor, and have a most comforting bedside manner. I wondered if he was a general practitioner, or if he worked in a hospital, and which part of the country he lived in.

I would no doubt find all this out this afternoon, and then I laughed at myself for the thought.

Really, I was almost as bad as Ben, wanting to know Peter Somerville's background in detail!

I rose from the bed with a final appraising look at my camellias, and went to pack my beach bag with all the impedimenta I would need for the afternoon's expedition to the Lido.

I tried to stuff my documents and other valuables into the only other handbag I had brought with me, but it was too small to accommodate everything, and in the end I decided not to cram it until it was out of shape, but instead to take my small jewel case to the hotel manager when I went down for lunch, and ask him to put it into his safe for me for the afternoon.

Since the linen costume I was wearing seemed to me to be rather formal wear for an afternoon

on the beach, after lunch I returned to my
bedroom to change.

In spite of all the rather grim and exciting
incidents of this past twenty-four hours, I was
feeling unusually gay and lighthearted at the
prospect of a lazy, peaceful afternoon at the
seashore, and to suit my mood, I put on an ex-
otically coloured dirndl skirt and wide-necked,
peasant-styled white cotton blouse, unpinned
my fair hair from the smooth, elegant French
roll style which I have adopted since I started
work, and let it ripple down to my shoulders in a
loose, casual page boy style.

A glance at my watch told me that Peter
would probably be already waiting for me in the
foyer, so quickly adding a touch of colour to my
lips, I snatched up my beach bag and went
blithely down to meet him.

Chapter Six

THERE WAS no sign of Peter in the foyer, but a glance at the clock above the reception desk indicated that my watch was at least a quarter of an hour fast. Rather than hang about the main hall, I went to sit in the lounge, which was actually a part of the hall, but separated from the main area by a glass partition and tubs of flowering oleanders and palm trees.

I had only been seated for a minute or two when a man and a woman entered the lounge and sat down on the adjoining settee.

I did not recognise them at first, and went on glancing through the fashion magazine I had picked up.

The man cleared his throat as if to attract my attention, and said, "Excuse me, it is Miss Lindsay, isn't it?"

I looked across at him with surprise and nodded.

"I do hope you have got over your frightening experience of last night," he went on. "It must have been horrifying for you to find poor Alice like that."

At his words I realised who this couple was, although seen clearly in the light of day, and without the strained, drawn appearance of last night, they both looked much younger than I had thought them to be. Last night I had taken them to be in their middle fifties. Today they looked ten years younger.

"It must have been dreadful for you, too," I said sympathetically. "Mrs. Sinclair was related to you, wasn't she?"

"She called me Sis, but she was really only my stepsister," explained Mrs. Lawrence. "She was seventeen when I was born and, understandably, although we were on quite friendly terms, we were never really close." Mrs. Lawrence took a cigarette from an elegantly slim gold case and inserted it into a long gold holder.

"As a matter of fact," she went on, "until she came on this European trip of hers, I hadn't set eyes on her since we came to live in Milan some twelve years ago. Now I wish she had never bothered to contact us!" The hand lighting the cigarette was shaking. "You see, I feel responsible in a way for what happened last night."

"Now, Betty!" Lawrence interrupted sharply, but his wife ignored him and continued.

"Alice was very keen to go down to Florence, but Harry said it would be much cooler in Venice at this time of year."

"No, my dear," protested her husband, unwilling to be involved in the blame. "I said that there was a heat wave in Florence just now, and you said there were as many museums and art galleries in Venice, and there was always the Lido for bathing if it got too hot."

"Yes, I know I said that, but wasn't it later? I would have quite liked to have gone to Florence, because they have some wonderful dress shops there, and there is a fabulous new one which that princess person has just opened—"

"And I reminded you, Betty, that Alice could not afford to buy anything there. She was doing this trip on a shoe string after saving for years to come here, and I said I did not think it would have been fair for you to go on a spending spree when she couldn't—"

"If she had sold that damned family jewellery of hers, instead of holding onto it for sentimental reasons, she would have been able to buy all the clothes she wanted, and she would not have been murdered either. She was always going on about it and someone must have heard her—"

"Now, Betty—"

I sensed that a good going family argument was about to ensue, and sighed with inward relief when I caught sight of Peter Somerville through the glass partition, standing beside the reception desk and talking to the girl there.

I excused myself, although I don't think either of them heard me, stood up and went to meet Peter.

The girl nodded in my direction as I approached, and Peter turned round.

"Hello, there!" he smiled as if he was genuinely pleased to see me. "I do hope I have not kept you waiting."

"My watch was fast, so I was a few minutes early," I smiled back at him.

"Here, let me carry that!" He took hold of my beach bag, then exclaimed at the weight.

"What on earth have you got in here? The Ducal jewels?"

He ushered me out of the hotel and we strolled across the Riva to the landing stage where the water bus for the Lido was already drawn up.

A couple of carabinieri were standing on either side of the gangway scrutinising the people who were embarking, but if they were looking for anyone in particular, they had a difficult job, because the passengers were pushing their way aboard, three and four abreast, and at one point I thought we would be wedged to a standstill.

The boat was so crowded there was scarcely room to breathe, but somehow Peter managed to manœuvre us towards the prow, where there was a little more elbow room.

I leaned against the rail regardless of the spray from the lagoon, which was whipped up by the bow of the boat as it cleaved its way through the wavelets, and blown into our faces by the gusty breeze which blew in from the Adriatic.

"Isn't it gloriously cool here!" I looked ahead of me, savouring the damp saltiness on my cheeks as we headed for the long, low bar of sand called the Lido.

"Don't you wonder how on earth these great hulking liners manage to evade all the sandbanks and dock in the Basin?" Peter's eyes followed the passage of a narrow funnelled cruise ship as it inched its way along the marked channel.

"They spoil the sky line," I objected. "I could hardly believe my eyes this morning when I saw a great high liner looming up off the Danieli." I shook my head. "It seemed quite incongruous."

I turned round to look back at the island city, with its pink and white palaces and golden domes and towering Campaniles all glittering in the afternoon sun.

"Isn't it unbelievably lovely!" I sighed. "I could come back here again and again and again, just for this view!"

Peter pursed his lips. "I agree Venice is very beautiful, but I prefer a beauty which is not man made. Craggy mountain peaks challenging the heavens, pine-covered hillsides, the incredible frozen loveliness of the Arctic wastes, sunlit Alpine meadows in the spring, with the first crocuses triumphing through the snow—to me these things are more splendid than this, lovely though I admit it to be."

I looked at him curiously.

"Where do you live, then, Dr. Somerville? In some remote mountain valley, I should imagine!"

He laughed. "If I had the choice, yes. But from necessity, or more truthfully, because I get more professional satisfaction from the work I do there, I have a general practice in the East End of London."

"You don't sound like a Londoner!" I was surprised.

"I'm not. I was born in Inverness, but my father's job took us to London. He was a lecturer at the University there. When I was eighteen I went back to Scotland to study medicine at St. Andrew's University, and then returned south." His eyes followed the flight of a bird which wheeled and swooped above our heads.

"I liked being at St. Andrew's. It was easy to get away from there at weekends to go skiing or climbing in the Cairngorms."

He turned to look at me again.

"I always took a summer vacation job in Scotland, to be near the mountains, and I had hoped to get a practice in Glasgow or Dundee, but as it happened I had to take what came my way, and so I live in London now."

"And no regrets?"

"For eleven months of the year I am too busy to have regrets."

"And the twelfth month?"

"On my annual holiday I usually go mountaineering or the like with a friend. This year is an exception," he gave a slight sigh. "For personal reasons I had to change my plans at the last moment, and come to Venice—but I am boring you with my life story, Miss Lindsay." His warm smile gave me a pleasurable feeling.

"No, you are not!" I denied positively. "And please call me Melanie," I asked. "Miss Lindsay sounds too formal for a holiday outing!"

His eyes twinkled. "Yes, Miss Lindsay does seem a bit formal for that gipsy outfit you are wearing, and your wind-blown hair. You remind me of—" he stopped and laughed. "I almost said Botticelli's Venus, but of course I meant that other girl of his—Primavera, with the flowers on her dress!"

The water bus had drawn up at the S. Maria

Elizabetta landing stage at the Lido, and was beginning to disgorge her passengers. We waited until almost everyone was off before moving to the gangway and strolling off onto the quayside, where two more carabinieri were standing on duty.

I looked at them, puzzled, and turned to Peter.

"Are there always policemen on duty at the landing stages?" I asked him.

"No. But they might be on the look out today for the man who attacked Mrs. Sinclair, or else there might be some truth in the rumour I heard at lunchtime, that there had been a political kidnapping last night!"

"A political kidnapping!" I gasped. "Venice seems to be a hot bed of crime. First last night's murder, then," I stopped in time. I did not want to mention the attempt to steal my shoulder bag even to Peter, "and then a kidnapping," I finished hastily. "I wonder if that is the reason Ben suddenly went off to Padua? It's the sort of story he would be interested in."

Peter had stopped listening to me and had stepped forward into the road to try to attract the attention of a taxi which was speeding in our direction.

"Where on earth are we going from here?" I asked.

"The bathing beach is on the other side of the island," he informed me, "and even if you feel energetic enough to walk there, I most certainly don't!" He smiled as he helped me into the cab.

"I never realised that there were any cars in Venice," I said as I sat down.

"The Lido isn't really Venice," said Peter. "All the same, I must admit I was rather surprised when I saw motor traffic here the first time I came."

He leant forward and told the driver to take us to the Grand Bathing Establishment, a title which made me raise my eyebrows in amusement.

The Gran Viale San Maria Elizabetta which leads across the island boasts some elegant shops, and I stared out at the passing scene with great interest.

When we reached the Adriatic side of the Lido we drove on along a seemingly endless esplanade with trees and gardens and modern hotels on one side, and rows and rows of beach cabins on the other—cabins which blocked our view of the sandy beach.

"Wasn't the Grand Hotel des Bains the background for Thomas Mann's famous novel, *Der Tod in Venedig?* I observed as I surveyed the hotel we were now passing with interest.

Peter nodded. "Venice seems to have attracted most of the famous poets and writers and artists of the world at some time in their lives, but Thomas Mann was the only one who made me feel the city was in some ways as repellent as it was beautiful."

"I didn't enjoy his book the first time I read it," I agreed.

"And the second time?" asked Peter.

I looked at him with surprise.

"How did you know I would read it again?"

He shrugged. "Perhaps because I did. You see, after reading it once, I found myself thinking about it so much, I had to re-read it, and this time old Aschenbach did not repel me at all. In fact I felt sorry for him."

"So did I!" I exclaimed, delighted that Peter had reached the same conclusion. "It made me wonder, too, if when I grow old, I shall try as desperately to recapture my lost youth as he did, or if I shall have the grace to accept old age as it comes."

"That is not a problem that you will be facing for some time yet!" Peter laughed. "And in any case, we haven't come here today to philosophise. We have come to enjoy ourselves!" he admonished me as the car came to a stop, and he helped me out.

We rented cubicles near the bath house and changed into our swim suits, and then went to look for a place on the brown sands on which to spread out our towels to sunbathe.

Eventually we found a space between a group of tall, lithe, suntanned, golden-haired Swedes, two girls and three young men who were playing an energetic game of volleyball, and an Italian family whose children were kneeling on the warm sand and happily piling the golden brown grit over the outstretched legs of their parents.

We sat down, and I took a tube of sun tan cream from my beach bag and applied it to my arms and legs. Peter gallantly offered to rub it on my back, and the firm yet gentle way he massaged the cream across my shoulders had a most relaxing effect.

"You have a very fair skin, Melanie," he observed as he screwed the cap back onto the tube. "You had better not lie too long in the sun today, or you could get badly burned. Ten minutes each side, and then we shall have a swim and look for a shady part to sit in."

"Yes, doctor!" I rolled over on my back and looked up at him, smiling.

In contrast to the creamy whiteness of my own skin, his was almost as brown as that of the bronzed Swedes who were larking about beside us, and I deduced that he must have been in Venice for a week or two, and was probably due to return home soon, which would be a pity, because it was a long time since I had felt so much at ease with someone I had met casually on holiday.

"When do you return to London, Peter?" I asked him.

"Not for another fifteen days," he said, "unless of course the locum who is standing in for me decides to throw in his hand. That happened once before, so keep your fingers crossed!"

The big beach ball with which our neighbours were playing came bouncing between us, and Peter flicked it lightly back. The taller of the two Swedish girls playfully hit it towards him again. Peter hadn't been prepared for this, and he was too late to stop the ball, which went sailing over his head, past the Italian children and their parents, and came down beside a lone sunbather on their other side—a small, thin man with dark sun glasses shielding his eyes, and a bald, gleaming, sunburned head.

He gave a grunt of annoyance as the ball bounced against him, sat up and angrily bounced it back at us, and then as if to underline his irritation, he turned his back on us.

The Swedish girl pouted in his direction, and I sat up and stared at him, or rather at his feet, which were unusually big for the size of him, and reminded me of diver's flippers.

They also reminded me of someone else, and I gave a sudden shiver of fear, then tried to laugh at myself for my silliness.

This could not possibly be the little man who had tried to steal my shoulder bag. He just could not be! Big feet and small stature were not the prerogative of one man!

I stole another quick glance at the bad tempered sunbather, but his back was still to us, and all I could see was his balding head and a birth mark on his neck, rather like a map of Italy in design.

Peter scrambled to his feet and joined in in the ball game with the Swedes and nudged me to do the same. I soon forgot about the other sunbather, and then after about a quarter of an hour of hectic exercise, we all went running down to the water's edge to cool off.

The sand was scorching under my feet, the sun scorching on my bare back, and we had to sidestep dozens of children who were paddling and splashing in the shallows, and dodge the many pedalloes, before the water was waist high and deep enough for swimming.

"Race you to the raft!" challenged Peter, plunging in pursuit of the Swedes who had reached the water before us.

I am not a powerful swimmer. It took me all my time to reach the floating square of wood which tossed on the water at a fairish distance, or so it seemed to me, from the shore, and I was so breathless by the time I reached it that Peter had to give me a helping hand to climb aboard.

I collapsed exhaustedly on the slippery planks, and lay there, gasping for breath and looking with dismay at the long stretch of water which lay between the raft and the shore, and which I would once more have to negotiate.

As I looked, a head bobbed up in the water a couple of feet from the raft, and I found myself staring directly down into a pair of ferret-like eyes, before the swimmer hurriedly turned to dive under the boards, but, as he did so, I caught sight of his neck, on which a purple map of Italy stood out with prominence.

Chapter Seven

IT IS a coincidence! I told myself fiercely. A coincidence! I was still hypersensitive after the shock of last night and the alarming experience of this morning, and this was making me look for spectres over my shoulder. Yes, that was the explanation.

And yet I shivered, as if the spectres I was denying had touched me with their icy fingers.

Peter, who had been talking to the pretty Swede who had inveigled him into the ball game, turned and saw my reaction.

"Melanie, are you cold?" he frowned.

I shook my head.

"You have had too much sun, that's what it is!" he said decisively. "I have been careless keeping you out in the open for so long on your first day."

"I am quite all right," I protested.

"You don't look all right," he persisted firmly. "I think we should get back to the shore and get changed.

I cast a suspicious glance among the heads bobbing between me and the shore.

Peter misinterpreted the look.

"Don't you think you can make it?" he asked.

"I should have warned you that I was not much of a swimmer," I said shakily.

"Not to worry!" He turned and murmured some words to one of the male Swedes. "We shall get you back safely!"

With Peter on one side, and the Swede on the other, I managed to reach shallow water somewhat laboriously. Our new friend returned to the raft, and Peter and I picked our way past the children at the water's edge and the sun worshippers lying on the sands.

Peter had a helping hand under my elbow to encourage me on my way, and as we moved forward he said apologetically:

"I am not much of a doctor, am I, giving you good advice one minute, then helping you to disobey orders the next!"

"It wasn't the sun which upset me," I denied. "It—" I stopped speaking as I went stumbling over a small sand-castle, causing its builder to howl with fury, and by the time I had made my abject apologies to the red-faced toddler, I had again changed my mind about telling Peter of the man who had snatched at my bag, and of whom I had been reminded by the bather who had been sitting near us on the beach.

"It was lack of sleep," I amended hastily.

"Or else last night's shock taking delayed effect," he surmised. "I think we should go back to the hotel now, and you should try to rest for a while."

We picked up our beach bags and towels and returned to the cabins to change.

When I came out to rejoin Peter, I could not

help taking a quick look round me, and when I saw that there was not a single small dark man with over-large feet in the vicinity, I decided that I had been letting my imagination go haywire on the beach, creating monsters where there were none, and I silently apologised to the man with the birth mark, whoever he might be, for vesting him with evil intentions!

We took a taxi back to the S. Maria Elizabetta landing stage, and were lucky enough to catch a ferry boat just as we arrived.

There were still carabinieri stationed at the landing stage, but they seemed more interested in who was arriving at the Lido than in who was leaving it, and they hardly spared us a glance.

At this time of day there were not many passengers and we were able to walk round the little ship, and get first-rate views of Venice from all sides.

"Peter, I am sorry to have spoilt your afternoon." I touched his arm as we leaned together against the guard rail at the prow.

He looked down at me. "I have enjoyed my afternoon," he said pleasantly. "I had intended to leave early in any case, as I have to meet a friend in the Piazza at six o'clock."

His dark eyes continued to scan my face.

"You still look a bit under the weather, Melanie. I think you should have an early night. I'll give you a couple of sedative pills to help you relax, if you wish."

I shook my head.

"I didn't come to Venice for early nights!" I told him. "In any case, I feel quite all right now.

I think it could have been the unaccustomed swim which upset me, but now I seem to have got my second wind!" I said lightly.

A motorboat, its side so highly polished that it reflected back the waters of the lagoon, drew up parallel with us and then went zooming past towards the Giudecca.

A breeze had blown up from the Adriatic, whipping the water into little, tossing waves which slapped against the side of the vessel, made my hair swirl in dishevelment against my face, and moulded my blouse and skirt round my body when I turned to face the gust to try to keep my hair out of my eyes.

After the searing heat which had scorched the Lido, I found this breeze invigorating, but the other passengers moved towards the lee side for shelter.

Peter said something to me, but his words were carried away by the wind, and I shook my head to indicate that I had not heard them.

He bent down to mutter them into my ear, but the rolling of the ship caught him unaware, and he overbalanced momentarily so that his lips brushed the lobe of my ear and touched my cheek, like a long caress.

He stepped back quickly, apologising for the moment of clumsiness, but again I did not hear the words he spoke, because the touch of his lips on my ear and cheek had had the most curious effect on me, setting my nerves aquiver as though they had been in contact with a live electric wire.

I gripped tightly at the guard rail to steady

myself both against the shock of this contact, and against another sudden dipping movement of the vessel as it turned round the marker buoy and made for the landing stage on the Riva degli Schiavonni.

Peter held out a hand to steady me, and again as his strong fingers gripped my arm, I felt the same peculiar sensation, as though the blood had drained from my head, leaving me dizzy.

Almost rudely I shrugged off his helpful hand, and bent down to pick up the beach bag I had placed at my feet.

Peter withdrew his hand, an odd expression on his face at my churlish movement, and without speaking, led the way to the side of the boat where the boatmen were waiting to slide the gangway into position.

We walked back to the hotel like indifferent strangers to whom even small talk is an effort, and I was glad to escape to the sanctuary of my room, where I busied myself washing out my swim suit and towel, having a bath, and washing and setting my hair for my evening date with Ben.

I kept trying to concentrate on all the things I wanted to ask Ben, and to tell him about, but invariably, to my annoyance, my thoughts would revert to Peter Somerville, and to wondering who it was he had to meet at six o'clock, and just why it was he had changed his mind and come to Venice on holiday instead of going mountaineering as he had originally planned.

The attraction which had brought him to

Venice must be very strong, I decided, to make him forgo his usual type of holiday.

I had a couple of hours to fill in before Ben was due to come for me, and possibly more, if he was late, as he had told Cerutti to tell me he might be.

I sat out on the balcony of my bedroom, overlooking the Riva, and let my hair dry in the still warm sun as I watched the passers-by beneath me go about their business.

I saw Peter leave the hotel just before six, but he was unaware of my scrutiny, and I followed the movement of his lithe figure as he strode along towards the Ponte della Paglia, but once he was out of sight I had a moment of unexpected depression, and retreated into the bedroom, where I sat in front of the dressing table and experimented with various hair styles to while the slow minutes away.

At seven o'clock I locked the window and drew the curtains and started to dress for my meeting with Ben. My black chiffon cocktail dress seemed the most appropriate thing to wear for my visit to Harry's Bar, and I clipped a black velvet choker, adorned with a gorgeous false topaz, which stressed the gold glints in my eyes, round my neck.

I brushed my hair out into the loose page-boy style which Peter had admired that afternoon, and, standing back to look at myself in the full-length wardrobe mirror, I decided I liked the effect.

There was still half an hour to go before Ben was due to call for me, and I prowled restlessly round the room, drawing aside the curtains to peer out of the side window and look down at the narrow waterway which separated the hotel from the neighbouring building.

The deepening shadows gave the scene an eerie, almost menacing aspect, and the sudden yowl of a cat fight starting up on the ledge somewhere beneath my window made me start back in fright, almost jerking the curtain off its railing with the movement, and making me decide that rather than stay up alone in my bedroom, and letting my too lively imagination hold sway, I would go down to the hotel cocktail bar and wait there for him.

The little bar was crowded. I recognised one or two of my fellow guests, and then at the right side of the counter I spotted Peter's dark head, and next to him the blonde girl I had seen him talking to after breakfast that morning.

I did not want him to see that I was on my own, and when I noticed the Lawrences about to enter the cocktail bar I waited until they were in the doorway and followed them in.

We managed to get seats beside the bar counter, and as I was sitting down, I caught sight of Peter watching me in the mirror behind the bottle display.

I ordered an aranciata and was paying for it when Peter came over to me and said:

"I thought I told you to get to bed early tonight."

I turned round casually and smiled at him.

"I have a date with Ben tonight, Peter, which will be much more of a tonic to me than a

night's rest! We are going to Harry's Bar," I
added inconsequentially.

"Peter! That's an idea! Let's go to Harry's
Bar too!" The fair girl was now standing beside
Peter, looking hopefully up at him.

"Not tonight, Chantal," he smiled down at
her, shaking his head. "Tomorrow, perhaps. I
have to wait here for a call from London,
remember."

She pouted prettily.

"I thought you came to Venice to forget
about work, Peter. Couldn't the receptionist
take the message for you?"

"Hardly," he replied dryly.

Chantal had been regarding me with every bit
as much interest as I had been looking at her,
and now, as if she did not want Peter to waste
time on any more pleasantries with me, she
tugged impatiently at his arm.

"Well, if you won't take me to Harry's Bar, let
us go and eat in the restaurant here. I am starv-
ing!"

Peter was not to be hurried.

Noticing the Lawrences seated beside me, he
asked Mrs. Lawrence how she was feeling, and if
she had been able to get a good night's sleep. As
he was speaking, Mr. Lawrence's eyes strayed
appreciatively over Chantal's blonde loveliness,
and she preened herself under his admiring
glance before once again giving Peter a
proprietory tug on the arm to make him follow
her.

I was beginning to feel somewhat sorry for
myself. Ben was late, and for that matter, might

not even turn up at all! It would not have been the first time this had happened, because with Ben his news story is first, last and everything in his life, and if there was any truth in what Peter had said about a political kidnapping, this was the kind of thing which would make Ben forget about everything but the job in hand.

"Are you on your own, Miss Lindsay?" asked Mr. Lawrence. "If you are, do join us."

"Thank you, I am waiting for a friend," I smiled at him.

"I still think you should have an early night, Melanie," said Peter seriously. "You did look pretty groggy this afternoon, you know."

"What is all this about my girl looking groggy?"

"Ben!" I whirled round with a joyous exclamation. "I was beginning to think you were not going to turn up!"

"And miss a date with you?" he put an affectionate hand on my shoulder. "Not on your life. Dates with you are too few and far between!" he eased himself onto an empty stool beside me. "What's that you are drinking? Still on orange juice?"

I nodded.

"One aranciata, one campari and soda, Pino," he said to the bartender. "And what for you two?" He turned to Peter and his girl friend.

"We were just about to leave, thanks all the same," said Peter, but the girl with him interrupted quickly.

"There is no hurry, Peter." She cancelled her

previous view as her eyes surveyed Ben with interest. "I should love a vermouth and soda."

Peter did not look too pleased at this change of mind. "Then I shall have the same, thanks." He turned to Ben.

"You haven't met Chantal Moodie, have you, Ferguson?" He introduced the blonde girl. "Chantal, this is Ben Ferguson, a friend of Melanie's," he stressed.

Chantal acknowledged the introduction with a charming smile at Ben before she said, glancing in my direction, "You have talked a lot about Melanie, Peter, but you have overlooked the formality of introducing us," she told him. "Or don't doctors introduce their patients to their friends?"

"Haven't you been well, Melanie?" Ben gave me an anxious look.

"Believe me, Ben, there is not a thing wrong with me. Dr. Somerville is being over solicitous." I looked coldly at Peter, annoyed by his persistence.

"Peter said that Melanie looked as if she was going to pass out on the raft at the Lido this afternoon." Chantal's great blue eyes were fixed on Ben's face as she spoke.

"If you want to know why that was, I'll tell you!" I flared up suddenly in annoyance at being made to appear frail and unable to spend an afternoon enjoying the sun.

"This morning I had rather a frightening experience. I decided to say nothing about it, because I did not want to have to face another barrage of police questions."

"What on earth are you talking about, Melanie?" asked Ben and Peter almost in unison.

I turned to Peter.

"Do you remember I told you that I thought I was being followed this morning?"

He nodded.

"Well, after I left you in the Piazza, to return to the hotel, the funny little man I had described to you tried to snatch my shoulder bag! He had actually cut through the strap which hung over my shoulder, when I happened to turn and catch him in the act. He promptly did a disappearing trick into the crowd."

"What!" gasped Peter. "Good Lord. Why didn't you go to the police straightaway?" he remonstrated angrily.

"What good would that have done?" I shrugged. "It wasn't as if he had actually stolen my bag, though he absolutely ruined it with his knife."

Ben caught at my arm and looked at me with narrowed eyes.

"Tell me your story from the beginning, Melanie," he ordered. "Who was this man you say was following you, and are you quite sure he was the man who later tried to steal your bag from you?"

"I am pretty observant, Ben, as I think you know. I happened to spot this man outside the hotel quite by accident. I actually bumped into him when I was returning to the hotel to get my camera. Then I noticed that he was never very far away when I stopped to take some snapshots," and I went on to explain to Ben how I had recognised him from the size of his feet and the pointed shoes, and how he had sat near me at the càfé in the Piazza, and how I had had no doubts at all that he was the one who had slashed at the strap of my bag.

"Quite a story, isn't it?" I finished with a shaky laugh, and took a sip of aranciata. "Oh, and there is one other thing. I still have his knife as a rather grim souvenir of the occasion. He left it sticking out of my bag!"

Chantal gasped, and Ben suddenly looked very grim and said determinedly:

"You will have to tell the police about this, Melanie."

"No," I said firmly. "I have had enough of police for the duration of my holiday here. I am not going to have it spoiled further."

"I still don't see what connection your story has with your taking ill on the raft in the afternoon!" objected Chantal.

I bit my lip, and looked indecisively at the interested faces round me.

"I know this sounds quite mad, and you will all laugh at me, but you see," I hesitated, "well I thought I saw the little bag snatcher again, on the beach at Lido!"

Chantal raised her elegant brows. "Yes, that does seem a bit far-fetched, doesn't it, Peter?"

Peter gave me a puzzled look.

"It does rather," he agreed. "I do think your nerves are getting the better of you, Melanie, and I don't wonder at it, after two very frightening experiences within such a short space of each other."

"Nerves, my foot!" I snapped angrily. "The two men were very alike, smallish, thinnish, dark skinned—"

"My dear Melanie," Ben smiled, "that description would fit about half the male population around here!"

"And do all the men in this part have outsize feet?" I asked acidly. "I told you the man who followed me in the morning had great big feet and long narrow shoes. The man on the beach had such big feet they looked like diving flippers!"

"I suppose that does narrow the field," agreed Ben. "Did you notice anything else about him?"

"Why, yes. There was one other thing. The man at the Lido had a peculiar birth mark on the back of his neck. It was shaped like the map of Italy. I noticed it first of all when he was lying on the beach, and then again when he swam out behind me to the raft. It was when I saw him bobbing up in the water only a couple of feet from where I was lying that I had my funny turn."

Peter was still unconvinced.

"I still think your nerves are making you over-suspicious of strangers. I mean to say," he glanced at Ben for confirmation, "is it likely that a sneak thief would keep dogging the same person? It isn't as if you were a well-known film star or the like, who might be carrying a fortune in jewellery round with you, and," he grinned suddenly, "he must have noticed that there wasn't much room for you to conceal your worldly wealth in that swimsuit you were wearing this afternoon!"

Oddly enough, Ben was not amused.

"I am going to have a word with Cerutti about this," he said firmly. "I don't like the sound of it."

"No! Please, Ben. I don't want any fuss."

"There will be no fuss, my dear. I shall merely describe this man you have been talking about to him and ask him if he knows a man with this uncommon birth mark. If such a man is not known at headquarters, I think you can rest assured that no one is dogging your footsteps, and you would like that assurance, wouldn't you?" He gave me a sympathetic look.

"I'll be back in a minute," he said, and eased himself off the bar stool to go over to the telephone booth.

"What does your friend do?" asked Chantal. "He seems to know his way around."

"Ben is a journalist," I replied curtly.

"Oh!" Her eyes widened with interest, and she glanced towards the telephone booth.

Peter ordered another round of drinks and was paying for them when Ben returned.

"What did Cerutti say?" I asked.

"He said he would look into it," replied Ben briefly, picking up the drink Peter had put before him.

"Peter?" Chantal took a sip of her vermouth. "If your telephone call comes through soon, and you don't want to take me to Harry's Bar, how about taking me for a ride in a gondola instead?"

Her eyes flirted with him. "There is a lovely moon tonight."

"I can recommend gliding down the Grand Canal in a gondola in the moonlight with a pretty girl!" twinkled Ben. "It is an essential ingredient for a holiday in Venice!"

"You sound like an old hand at the game, Ben!" I teased him, lighthearted now that we had stopped talking about my misadventures that day." Perhaps it was you I saw go gliding past my window last night in a gondola, leering down at a gorgeous blonde!"

"Not guilty this time, Melanie," he laughed. "I was working until the small hours in my bedroom last night, on my latest story."

"Come to think of it," I said slowly, "the Don Giovanni in the gondola was not like you. He was a bit older." I eyed Ben's square, strong frame. "And yet," I frowned, "in a way he did remind me of someone I have met."

"Not your bagsnatcher again!" sneered Chantal.

"N-no." I was too busy trying to recapture an elusive memory to notice the sneer. "Now, what was it about him?" I frowned.

"Come on, my dear, drink up!" Ben chivvied me. "You can think about your Don Giovanni some other time, but meantime, if we don't get along to Harry's Bar soon, we shall never get a table."

Chapter Eight

THE AFTERNOON breeze which I had enjoyed as we sailed across the lagoon had died away and the night air was hot and still.

At Ben's suggestion I had gone to my room for a shawl to drape over my shoulders, since he had advised me that the night air could be damp and treacherous, but at the moment I had no need of it, and I carried it with my slim gold evening bag in my left hand as we strolled along the quay, over the Ponte della Paglia and along to the San Marco Ferry stop which is almost opposite Harry's Bar.

Above the entrance to the restaurant hung an illuminated cocktail shaker, and we passed underneath the sign into a crowded room.

Until this moment I had never realised how many people could be packed into an enclosed space without suffocating. Sardines in a tin had more room to themselves, I decided, and I wondered if Ben was going to make what seemed to me to be a hopeless effort to get to the bar counter.

He seemed to think it was worth a try, for he turned to me, smiling encouragement.

"Follow me, Melanie, but forget your party manners for the next few seconds, until we reach the bar!" he advised, and proceeded to furrow a passage through the chattering groups of people who were standing at least three deep round the counter.

By some miracle we achieved our object, although once we had, I wondered if there was enough elbow room there to raise a glass!

"What will it be, Melanie, a Titian or a Giorgione?" Ben asked with a grin.

"A what?" I gaped at him. "Do you mean to say they sell pictures here as well?"

Ben's grin widened, and a young man who was wedged against him at the bar somehow managed to look round at me with amused eyes as Ben explained.

"Titians and Giorgiones are the special cocktails they mix for you here. Would you like to try one?"

"Oh! Oh, I see." I hesitated. "How potent are they?"

"For a girl brought up like you on orange juice, they might be quite heady, but one would do you no harm. In fact," he smiled at me, "it might help you to relax after the trying day you have had. Yes," he decided. "A Titian for you it shall be, young lady!"

He turned to the barman to give his order, and I swivelled on my stool to take an interested look at the people crowding round me.

The air was thick with the smoke of cigars and cheroots and cigarettes, which the whirring ventilators did their best to disperse and redolent of expensive perfumes and after-shave lotions.

I was fascinated by the scene, because there

were so many different types, so many different nationalities packed into such a limited space.

The noise of voices would have made Babel seem a city of silence, and I wondered how anyone could follow a conversation.

In my left ear a shrill-toned Frenchwoman was relating that she had a wonderful little dressmaker back home in Paris, who would make a superlative evening gown for her from the length of silk she had bought that afternoon at Rubelli's.

In my other ear, an American twanged.

"I bought Johnnie a couple of silk shirts at the Cameceria just a few steps up the Calle from here. They are absolutely out of this world. The Venetians know a thing or two about quality, don't they?"

While she waited for her answer an English voice sounding very clear and precise in a sudden lull of talk said:

"I wonder if there is any truth in this story of a political kidnapping?" He looked down with maudlin gaze at the lovely, sloe-eyed beauty he was with. "It doesn't seem possible, does it, a kidnapping in Venice? In any case, there has not been a word of confirmation in the late papers or on the radio."

Ben nudged me to tell me that my drink was on the counter.

"Don't dare spill any of it!" he warned me. "At the price I paid for it, gold must be the main ingredient!"

He raised his own glass and clinked it against

mine. "Cheers, my dear! And down with big-footed villains!"

I smiled and took a sip of the cocktail.

"Mmmmm!" I murmured approvingly. "It is nice!"

I took another sip, and then asked him:

"Ben, have you heard anything about this kidnapping everyone seems to be talking about?"

"Wherever you get a mob of idlers, you always get a lot of gossip and rumour," he evaded the question.

"It was Peter who first mentioned it to me this afternoon." I looked at him suspiciously. "He said it might explain the presence of so many carabinieri at the landing stages. Are you sure there is nothing to the story?"

"I wonder where Peter got hold of it?" Ben frowned.

"Everybody has got hold of the kidnapping story, Ferguson." A wizened, little man in a white dinner jacket insinuated himself between my stool and where Ben was standing, and turned to look at me with flattering admiration. Still looking at me, he went on, "As a newsman, I am surprised that you are not snooping around the Questura to find out if it is true or not."

"Who is supposed to have been kidnapped?" I asked him.

"I heard someone say that it was Martin Radcliffe's daughter." The sharp-eyed little man transferred his gaze from me to Ben. "Are you sure you cannot confirm that?" he pried.

Ben's expression did not change, and if I had

not known him so well, I would not have realised that he was trying to hide something, but I saw the irritated way his little finger beat against the glass he was holding, and the way he shrugged his shoulders with a too indifferent gesture, and I knew he was in possession of some facts about the kidnapping he did not want to divulge.

"Where on earth do you get all your stories from, Vernon?" he asked lightly. "The newsboy in St. Mark's Square or the barman at the Pilsen?"

"Then it isn't true?" persisted the man in the white dinner jacket. "Can I quote you on that?"

"For goodness sake!" I exclaimed suddenly, diverting his attention. "Don't make Ben think he is missing out on a story. He is supposed to be wining and dining with me this evening, but if he thought there was something in what you have been saying, he would leave me high, dry and hungry!"

I did not imagine the look of relief on Ben's face at my tactics, and before the other could return to his verbal attack, Ben said smoothly:

"Our table is free now, Melanie. We had better go and claim it."

"And I am ready to sample all those wonderful dishes I have heard this place is noted for!" I slipped down from the bar stool. "If they are as good as the Titian was, they will be memorable!"

We elbowed our way through to the dining area, and a table for two, beside which a waiter was hovering.

"Good evening, Signor Ferguson," he greeted Ben as he held out a chair for me to sit down.

I was handed the menu card, but after a fleeting glance at it I shook my head and said to Ben:

"I think I had better let you choose. You seem to know about the dishes here, and you also have some idea of my likes and dislikes, although," I gave another glance at the printed card, "*Fritto Misto* could be wonderful, and *capitone* a dream. On the other hand, they might merely be names to cover my pet hates!"

After due consideration, Ben gave the order, and his choice proved two things. That although it was some time since we had seen each other, he had not forgotten my likes and dislikes, and also that Venetian dishes, cooked as they had been cooked by the chef of Harry's Bar, are as good as any gourmet could hope to taste anywhere in the world.

By the time I had spooned up the last rich morsel of *Cassata Siciliana* I felt sated and sleepy, and willing to linger over the strega which Ben had ordered with the coffee.

I sighed with contentment.

Ben looked at me and smiled.

"You will not need any of Dr. Somerville's pills to send you to sleep tonight," he observed. "You look as satisfied and relaxed as a well-fed cat!"

"Now that is what I call a pretty compliment, Ben!" I managed to stifle a yawn. "Oh dear! I do feel sleepy. Let's go for a walk in the moonlight to wake me up again!"

"Our walk in the moonlight will be straight from here back to your hotel, Melanie, my love," said Ben firmly.

"Tonight I must agree with your doctor friend. An early night is what you are most in need of!"

He signalled the waiter, paid the bill, and we were on the point of leaving when Cerutti, the police captain, appeared in the doorway.

When he spotted us, he came directly across the room.

"I was told I would find you here," he announced. "I am glad I did."

"Was there something you wanted to see me about?" frowned Ben.

Cerutti nodded, and gave a glance around him.

"It is rather crowded here for me to talk to you," he observed.

"We were just about to leave," Ben told him. "I was going to take Signorina Lindsay back to her hotel."

"Then I shall walk with you." The policeman stood aside to let us precede him from the restaurant.

It was after ten, but there was still a lot of movement on the quay. Couples meandered along, hand in hand, shoulders touching, looking into each other's eyes, aware of no one but themselves. A pack of trippers who had newly disembarked from the vaporetto at the San Marco landing stage chattered to each other about the excursion they had just made, their voices shrill as sparrow song in the still night air.

Moonshine and lamplight mingled and intermingled as they reflected back from the eerily black water of the lagoon, and across the water the lights of the Giudecca, and beyond that, in the distance, the lights of the Lido, were strung like ropes of shimmering pearls against the night sky.

Ben slipped his arm through mine, and I clung to it sleepily, wishing that Captain Cerutti would hurry up and say what he had been so anxious to say to Ben, and then go off and leave us on our own to enjoy Venice by moonlight.

"Signor Ferguson." Cerutti fell into step beside us. "You telephoned me earlier this evening to ask me about a certain man?"

"Yes?" Ben's grip on my arm tightened in warning.

"Just why are you interested in this particular man, signor? Had you heard anything about him?"

"Have you found out who he is?" Ben countered question with question.

"We have found the man himself!" replied Cerutti.

"Oh!" I could not stifle my sudden gasp of surprise.

Cerutti gave me a suspicious look.

"Did you know this man, signorina? Had you seen him somewhere?" he demanded sharply.

I looked towards Ben for guidance.

"I think you should tell Captain Cerutti the story you told me earlier this evening, Melanie," said Ben gravely. "Start from the moment when you saw him first of all."

"But—"

"No buts," he said firmly. "From the expression on the captain's face, I think you could be in trouble if you don't co-operate!"

I gave a nervous shudder and drew my gaily-embroidered shawl more tightly round my shoulders.

"The more I think of it, the more stupid it seems." I was unwilling to begin my recital.

"Let me be the judge of that, signorina," said Cerutti.

"Well, it was like this," I began, and when I had finished the tale, which sounded more and more senseless on the retelling, I said, with a touch of bravado:

"Now, tell me, Captain Cerutti, which of my two admirers have you tracked down for me? The one who was really only interested in stealing my bag, or the man on the Lido who was interested in me even when I had nothing worth stealing, or do they happen to be one and the same person?"

We had already reached the Ponte della Paglia and at the foot of the steps Cerutti stopped.

"As you had surmised, signorina," said the captain gravely, "there was only one man following you today, and not only do we have a record of this man at the Questura, but he is also wanted by Interpol. He has a record of violence in New York, Vienna, Naples and Milan, and he is believed to have a connection with the Mafia.

He is wanted in Milan for murder, and it is known that he can be hired, at a price, to commit any crime he is asked!"

I clutched hard at Ben's arm, and the world seemed suddenly to be made up of dancing moons and swaying lights, which merged into a giant whirling ball of glaring brightness which was about to explode.

"It is all right, signorina!" Cerutti's anxious voice seemed to come from a long way away. "You will have nothing to worry about any more. This man, Eduardo Conti, will not give you further trouble."

"So you have him under lock and key? Good!" Ben's calm voice, the reassuring pressure of his hand on my arm, helped drag me back from the world of vertigo, and slowly the lights stopped spinning round, the moon ceased to whirl and remained motionless in the night blue sky, and I was myself again.

"Yes, we have got him."

There seemed to be a note of dissatisfaction in Cerutti's voice which made me give him a puzzled look.

He went on slowly: "When we found Conti, he still had in his possession one of the rings and a pair of earrings belonging to the Signora Sinclair—"

"So he was the man who killed her!" I interrupted him with a cry of amazement.

"It would not be the first time he had killed his victim in furtherance of his crimes," said Cerutti soberly. "He held life cheaply, signorina, and because he must have thought you had seen him leave the Signora Sinclair's bedroom, or even seen him in the corridor when you went hurrying to see what was wrong with her, he decided that as far as he was concerned, the best witness was a dead one!"

I drew in a sharp breath.

"Conti was not trying to steal your bag this morning, Signorina Lindsay," went on Cerutti. "He was waiting for an opportunity to stick a knife into your back!" The captain certainly did not believe in mincing words. "Fortunately for you, by a miracle your bag got in the way of his blade at the first attempt, and in the afternoon, at the Lido, no opportunity to get you presented itself."

"Thank God you have him in safe keeping now!" said Ben with heartfelt relief in his voice. "I suppose one of your men spotted him at the Lido when they were on the lookout for—" he stopped short and Cerutti smoothly interrupted him.

"As a matter of fact, no. A gondolier spotted him in a rio less than an hour ago, and reported to us."

Captain Cerutti turned to me. "Eduardo Conti is dead, signorina. A drunken brawl, at a guess, when he was knocked out and probably rolled into the water, was a fitting end for him, so you see," he went on, "you need worry no more about the unwanted attentions of a little man with big feet!"

"And you have had a nasty crime satisfactorily wound up," said Ben. "You will be glad that the murderer of Signora Sinclair has been found."

"Yes!" said Cerutti abruptly. "I am glad of that. It leaves me free to give all my attention to my other case."

He gave a smart salute.

"Enjoy the remainder of your holiday in the Serenissima with a light heart, signorina. *Buono notte, signorina, signore.*"

He turned on his heel and left us to return to the hotel on our own.

Chapter Nine

THE TALK with Cerutti had banished my sleepiness and left me with such a feeling of light-hearted relief that I now no longer wanted to return sedately to my hotel and go early to bed.

"Isn't there somewhere else we can visit?" I begged Ben. "What about the Casino?" I asked gaily. "I was told there was one in Venice, and I think this could be my lucky night!"

I smiled up into Ben's face. "You have no idea how wonderful it is to feel that I was right, and it was no nervous persecution mania I had about thinking that man was following me around, and better still to know that he will never bother me, or anyone else, again."

Ben was adamant.

"You are right about there being a Casino, my dear, and if I am free tomorrow night, I shall certainly take you there to try your luck, but not tonight!" he shook his head. "Yes," he went on, "I can guess exactly how you are feeling at the moment, but the mood won't last. This new-found exhilaration will collapse like a bubble in about half an hour, and I would be a poor friend if I gave in to you. No," he said firmly, "it is early to bed for you tonight!"

"You sound just like my father!" I pouted.

"I don't feel like a father to you, heaven forbid!" His eyes twinkled, and he gave my arm an affectionate squeeze, "but for once I shall act in *loco parentis*! It is not that I want to be rid of you for the rest of the evening, Melanie, but I am thinking of your own good."

"But I feel so wide awake now!" I wailed. "I shall never fall off to sleep if I go to bed now!"

"I wonder if you will say that after you have tried one of Pino's nightcaps?" mused Ben, pushing open the glass door of the hotel and leading the way to the cocktail bar to the left of the hall.

The bar was still very busy. Peter was standing at the counter with Chantal and two tall, handsome, young Italians, one of whom I recognised as Captain Cerutti's assistant. Out of uniform, he seemed much more sure of himself and less restrained and the way he was ogling Chantal would have made me furious if she had been my girl, although Peter seemed more amused than infuriated at his behaviour.

Chantal waved to us as we came in, and beckoned to us to join them.

"Wasn't it a pity, Peter's telephone call did not come through until half an hour ago." She shook her head in mock pity. "So I did not get my gondola ride with him after all. Still," her eyes flirted with her two new companions, "the evening has been fun all the same."

She waved her hand towards the two Italians.

"This is Carlo Benvenuto and this is Mario Valdi. They want to practise speaking English, although Carlo speaks almost as well as I do, so I have been giving them lessons, isn't that right, Peter?"

He nodded, giving me an amused wink as he did so.

"They are also trying to improve my Italian," she went on, with a mischievous smile, "but they will have to give me a good many lessons, or so they say!"

Carlo and Mario, acknowledging her casual introduction, stood up to let me have one of the bar stools, and I wriggled up on to the one beside Chantal.

"Melanie," she addressed me, "I was telling Carlo about the man you said was following you. You didn't mind, did you? He says this happens all the time, because English women in Italy seem to expect it."

"Well, I didn't, and I didn't like it either," I retorted sharply. "However, that particular pest will not be annoying me again. He is," I hesitated as I saw a warning look flash in Ben's eyes, "he is at present under police surveillance," I concluded truthfully.

When I had finished the cocktail Ben had ordered for me, he firmly insisted I went to my room, and to make sure that I obeyed him, he accompanied me right to my bedroom door, and opened it for me.

Before I went into the room, he gripped my shoulders with both hands and looked at me steadily.

"Play it safe, Melanie, my dear. Don't forget to turn the key in the lock and bolt the door and the windows," he advised me as he bent down to brush my cheek with his lips in a more fraternal than loverly caress. "Eduardo Conti is not the only thief in Venice, as Cerutti well knows!"

He waited outside the door until he heard me turn the key in the lock, then called "Good-night."

I listened to the sound of his departing footsteps and, following his advice, checked carefully to see that the windows were securely bolted, and then quickly undressed and slipped into bed, aware that the sleep which I had been fighting off for the greater part of the evening was beginning to win the struggle.

I stretched my hand up and pulled the cord which extinguished the bedside light, and the next thing I knew, I was being rudely awakened by the ringing of the telephone at my bedside.

"*Pronto!*" I murmured sleepily into the mouthpiece as I raised myself up on one elbow on the bed.

"It is Peter Somerville, Melanie. You sound as if you are still half asleep!"

"Of course I am half asleep!" I exclaimed indignantly. "What on earth are you calling me for in the middle of the night?"

Peter's amused laugh across the wires almost deafened my poor ears. "Since when has half past nine in the morning been the middle of the night?" he asked.

I looked at my bedside clock and sat bolt upright.

"Peter! It can't be! It seems only seconds since I got into bed!"

"Then either you have been up all night or else you have been enjoying the kind of sleep the doctor ordered!" he said, the laughter still in his voice. "How long will it take you to get dressed?" he went on.

"Ten minutes, quarter of an hour," I replied. "Why?"

"I thought you might like to see some of the countryside around Venice while you are here, and I have my car parked at the causeway."

"That sounds a wonderful idea!" I began enthusiastically, then added, more slowly, "but Ben said he would get in touch with me sometime today."

"I very much doubt if Ben will have any free time today," said Peter more soberly. "These rumours that were rife all over Venice yesterday about a kidnapping have turned out to be true. Lauren Radcliffe, the financier's daughter, has been missing from her hotel room for over twenty-four hours. Every policeman in the area has been alerted, and the newsmen are gathering here in force. Ferguson could not miss out on a story like this."

"No," I said slowly. "He couldn't."

Even as I was speaking I was thinking of the tight, closed, give nothing away look that Ben had worn last night when the man in the white dinner jacket had asked him to confirm the story. I was fairly sure that at that particular time, Ben had known about the kidnapping, but had perhaps been warned by the police to say nothing until official permission was given.

He and the police captain, Cerutti, seemed to be on good terms, and to respect each other's job, so I was not surprised he had acted as he had done, not even giving me a hint of what he knew.

"Then how about coming with me today?" urged Peter. "We could get as far afield as Lake Garda, or even north as far as Cortina, if we leave fairly soon. The choice is yours."

I was about to say, "What about Chantal?" but I refrained, although it did seem odd, considering how friendly they appeared to be, that he was asking me, and not the pretty young blonde, to go with him today.

"I shall leave the choice up to you," I told him. "Both places sound equally delightful. You can let me know your decision when I meet you in the foyer in about ten minutes."

"Bring your bathing gear and a warm jacket with you. That way you will be prepared for whichever place I decide to go to," he advised me. "And now, I shall go and order breakfast for you before the waiters go off duty!" he said cheerfully. "Don't be too long, or the coffee will get cold!"

I dressed in record time in a lightweight white wool sleeveless dress, with a jacket to match, tied a gold scarf pirate fashion round my hair, hurriedly put all the gear I would need for the day's outing into a small handgrip, and went down to the breakfast room, where Chantal had joined Peter at a table for three.

Chantal was looking sulky and I wondered if she objected to my going with Peter. However, the reason for her sulkiness was soon explained when she told me that her own plans for the day had fallen through, because she had been going to spend it on the Lido with Carlo Benvenuto, and now his day off had been cancelled because of the kidnapping of Radcliffe's daughter, and her outing to the Lido had been called off.

"So now I shall just have to come to Cortina with you," she muttered with a pout, "and Cortina is not at all my cup of tea at this time of year. I much prefer swimming to scrambling round mountain tops in the summer!"

"All right, you win," said Peter good humouredly. "We shall go to Lake Garda instead. You will get the swimming you want there, so off with you and pack your things, while Melanie has her breakfast."

When she left us, beaming with delight at having got her own way, I said to Peter:

"Look, Peter, now that Chantal is free to go with you, do you still want me to come along? I don't want you to feel you have to take me—"

"Of course I want you to come with me!" Peter seemed surprised at my words. "I would not have asked you if I hadn't. It's too bad Chantal's arrangements were upset, but it is high time she learned that she cannot always have what she wants. She is a thoughtless, selfish, self-centred young woman at times," said Peter with acerbity, "and, indeed, if it wasn't for her, let me tell you, I would not have been within a hundred miles of Venice this summer!

What makes me mad at times," he gave a rueful smile, "is that half the time I might as well not be here, while she goes her own sweet way!"

"She is still young," I said from the advantage of my few years' seniority. I wanted to find an excuse for Chantal's selfish behaviour, and yet at the same time I felt annoyed with her for Peter's sake, because she did not seem to appreciate that he had sacrificed his own holiday plans to accommodate her. I also felt annoyed with Peter himself, for letting himself be twisted round the little finger of this pleasure-seeking young woman. He must be genuinely infatuated by her, I decided, not to object to the way she delighted in flaunting her other conquests under his nose, but his next words indicated that he was not so insensitive to her behaviour as I was beginning to imagine.

"Youth is an excuse for too much thoughtlessness these days," he said with a flash of annoyance. "It is high time Chantal learned to be less selfish and possessive, as if the world owed her a living. I am beginning to realise what her mother was talking about when she said she hoped I knew what I was taking on!"

His last words made me feel quite depressed. To begin with, I had thought that he and Chantal were mere holiday friends, but from what he was saying now, it would appear that their relationship was much closer than that.

Why, then, had he invited me to go out with him today? Had he wanted to show Chantal that two can play at the same game? I did not like the feeling of being a pawn rather than a player, and I shot Peter a covert look.

Although Ben had cast vague doubts in my mind about him, I had decided to take Peter Somerville at my own assessment, and until this moment, that assessment had been high.

Now I was beginning to wonder if his charm had blinded me to his weakness of character, and I very nearly resolved to tell him that after all I could not spend the day with him. However, I could not think of an easy way out of the situation, and before I could work out a plausible excuse, Chantal returned, looking enchanting in a pale blue cotton dress, tightly belted round her minute waist, and with her fair hair tied in a pony tail with a pale blue, chiffon scarf.

"Here I am!" she announced unnecessarily. "I hope you have finished breakfast, Melanie," she went on, "because from my window I saw a motoscafo approaching the landing stage, and if we hurry we should catch it."

It was my first trip down the Grand Canal by daylight, and I was completely entranced by it. Peter pointed out the various buildings of note as we sailed past them, and as we approached the Rialto Bridge, I tried to get a snapshot of it, but one of the boatmen walked in front of me at the critical moment, and all I got for my pains, since I had actually clicked the lever, was a shot of a blue and white striped cotton shirt!

"Never mind," Peter consoled me. "At least you have an original photograph of Venice, and in any case, there is plenty of time for you to get all the photographs you want of the city. You have another twelve days here, haven't you?"

I nodded.

"We have another fourteen," announced Chantal, "but I have seen all the buildings and art galleries and insides of churches I want to see, and intend to spend the rest of my stay at the Lido, acquiring a tan."

"Showing off your tan, you mean!" retorted Peter.

She ignored him as her eyes followed the progress of a black gondola.

"Have you ever been in a gondola, Melanie?" she asked.

I shook my head. "This is my first visit to Venice."

"It is a wonderful experience!" she said with enthusiasm, "Peter, you will have to arrange to take Melanie in one," she suggested magnanimously. "Preferably by moonlight!" she giggled. "It was fun last night with Carlo and Mario. Mario has such a fine singing voice, and he knows the most romantic ballads!"

"You will find yourself in trouble one of these days, young lady, if you go gallivanting in gondolas with strangers. I thought you had gone to your room when you left the cocktail bar last night."

"I asked you to take me out in a gondola, and you said it was too late," she challenged him. "So when Carlo and Mario offered to take me, I did not see why I should not go with them. After all," she giggled, "Carlo is a policeman, and who should be able to look after one better than a policeman?"

Peter gave her an exasperated look.

"Thank goodness your mother does not know half the things you get up to!"

"Mother knows that you will see I come to no harm," Chantal teased him. "And in any case, I am eighteen now, and well able to look after myself. Not that Mother could talk!" she went on. "She wasn't much older than me when she eloped with Father when she was in her first year at University!"

"I don't think she wants history to repeat itself," said Peter dryly.

"She will be glad to get me off her hands!" laughed Chantal. "She and I are too alike to live under the same roof!"

I listened to their good-natured banter, feeling very much out of it, and wishing more and more that I had made that last-minute decision not to come on this outing with them, and, when Chantal caught hold of Peter's hand to draw his attention to a house on the left side of the canal, from whose upper balcony cascaded a thick mass of purple wistaria blooms, I felt almost breathless with an inexplicable sensation of jealousy at the gesture, and I turned away from them to gaze blindly back down the canal, and try to analyse the peculiar emotion.

When we reached the Piazzale Roma, everyone shoved and jostled one another in their haste to disembark.

Peter grabbed Chantal and me by the arm, so

that we wouldn't be separated from each other in the crush, and somehow we squeezed safely off the gangway.

We made for the large garage at the end of the causeway where Peter had parked his car for the duration of the stay in Venice.

It was odd to find oneself back amid the hustle and bustle of motorised street traffic again after two days in Venice's motorless quays and calles, and I found it even more odd than the other two, who were used to motoring on the Continent, because I could not get the hang of watching out for traffic coming from what with British insularity I referred to as "the wrong side."

Peter let go of our arms, and told us to wait for him while he dashed across the road to buy a later edition of the morning paper from the news kiosk.

Chantal and I obediently stood on the edge of the pavement to wait for him, and to watch with fascinated eyes the speed of the traffic, from Vespas to large touring coaches, which went whizzing past us along the causeway.

"Look!" Chantal grabbed my arm. "There is a coach with G.B. plates. Let's give it a wave!" she cried with childish enthusiasm, raising her hand in a gay gesture.

I was about to follow suit, when someone jostled roughly against my back, and sent me teetering off balance into the path of an approaching bus.

A woman beside me screamed, and then my

arm was gripped by strong young fingers as Chantal grabbed me and pulled me back on to the pavement only seconds before the coach went thundering past us.

Chapter Ten

CHANTAL AND I clung shakily to each other for a minute or two, deaf to the excited chatter which had started to buzz around us.

Italians love to make a drama of every small incident in life, and if I had not been so shaken I would have been amused at the pantomimic gesticulations and the turbulent flow of language from the people standing nearby, who were pulling at my arm, and trying to indicate exactly what had happened, but my few words of Italian did not even get the gist of what they were trying to say.

"Let's get away from here," I muttered to Chantal. "I hate being the centre of attention!"

"They are making an awful song and dance about it," she agreed. "That old woman is even saying you were deliberately pushed!"

I groaned. "Not again! Give me Venice for masses of excitement any day!"

Chantal giggled, and somehow we managed, with actions as gesticulatory as of those surrounding us, to explain that there had been no harm done, and that we had to be on our way.

Fortunately Peter had not noticed the actual incident from where he was standing at the entrance to the enormous garage where his car was parked.

"What was all the excitement in your direction about?" he asked, mildly interested, as we joined him.

"The usual Italian storm in a teacup," I replied evasively, giving Chantal a warning look not to go into details.

"Life is never dull in this country, is it?" Chantal cheerfully followed her cue. "These Italians live every moment of it to the full. No incident seems too slight for them to transform into high drama!"

We followed Peter to his car, a white B.M.W., which proved to be very speedy and comfortable as we drove along the flat, almost dead-straight autostrada which leads from Mestre to the Italian Lakes and Milan.

The countryside was not particularly interesting at this part, and seated as I was in the back passenger seat, instead of looking out at the passing scene, I found my eyes straying to watch Peter Somerville's profile, and I wondered whether I had indeed misread his character, and what his relationship was to the pretty, gay young woman by his side. Somehow I did not see her settling down as the wife of a busy general practitioner in London's dockland.

Chantal's inconsequential chatter distracted my attention.

She talked about the various people she had met in the hotel, about the fascinations of Carlo and Mario, and then she went on: "I did not see

the Lawrences at breakfast this morning, did
you, Peter?"

"They have left the Hotel Capri," answered
Peter. "I believe Lawrence has gone back to
Milan about some business matter that has
cropped up, and that Betty Lawrence has
decided to stay in another hotel until the
funeral arrangements for her sister are com-
pleted. She said that she simply could not bear
to stay on alone in the Capri after what had
happened."

"That is her story!" sneered Chantal. "Personally I think she was glad of an excuse to get
away to another hotel. I mean to say, everyone
was amused at the panic she was thrown into
when her husband arrived so unexpectedly last
week, and interrupted her fun and games with
the handsome Carlo!"

"Didn't Mr. Lawrence arrive in Venice with
his wife and her sister?" I asked in surprise.

Chantal turned round to look at me.

"I had forgotten you had only been at the
Capri for a couple of nights, so you wouldn't
know the story!" she laughed. "It caused quite a
bit of talk among the other hotel guests, and it
was obvious that poor Mrs. Sinclair was not at
all happy about the situation, but what could
she say? After all, in a way, it was she who was
responsible for her sister's meeting with Carlo."

"Chantal!" protested Peter. "That is all water
under the bridge. There is no need to gossip
about it now."

"Fiddle dee!" Chantal tossed her head impudently. "Melanie would not be a true female if she didn't enjoy a bit of gossip."

Ignoring Peter's interruption, she turned back to me to resume her story.

"You have probably gathered from the course of events that Mrs. Sinclair was one of the worrying kind—about money, about her jewels, about sneak thieves and so on. Well, the very day they arrived at the hotel, she mislaid her cheque book and wallet. At the time, she was so sure they had been stolen that she insisted on calling in the police. Carlo, who speaks excellent English, even if he insists he needs practice," she added, giving Peter a sly smile, "was sent along to the hotel from the Questura in mufti, at the proprietor's request, to look into the matter. By the time he arrived, needless to say the cheque book and wallet had been found. Because Mrs. Sinclair felt foolish at her hasty action in calling the police, she asked her sister to make her apologies to the police for her.

"You have seen Carlo, Melanie." Chantal's eyes held a dreamy expression. "He is tall, he is dark, he is very good-looking, and with more sex appeal even than Frank Sinatra in his heyday and with those beautiful manners which make a girl feel she is being treated like a princess, he attracted Mrs. Lawrence.

"Actually," she said thoughtfully, "Betty Lawrence is not at all bad looking for a woman nudging forty, if she hasn't actually elbowed into her fourth decade, and she let Carlo know that she was attracted to him.

"I expect it flattered his vanity in a way to

have a rich, sophisticated woman take an interest in him, and they started going out together, with Mrs. Sinclair sadly trailing along with them from time to time, but more often they were on their own, because Mrs. Sinclair used to go to her room after dinner in the evenings, on the excuse that her doctor had told her she was to get plenty of rest, although most people thought that it was because she could not afford to live up to her sister's standard of entertainment, don't you agree, Peter?"

Peter said nothing, but his expression, as he concentrated on the road ahead was tight-lipped, as if he did not want to be associated with Chantal's idle chatter.

Chantal winked at me, not in the least perturbed by his attitude, and went on with her story.

"Then Harry Lawrence turned up out of the blue, and this put an end to his wife's little affair. I sometimes wonder," she mused, "if Mrs. Sinclair was getting so fed up with her sister for leaving her alone so much, that she sent for him to come here!"

"Poor Mrs. Lawrence!" I said with a degree of sympathy. "It must have been most embarrassing for her when Carlo turned up again as one of the officers investigating her sister's death."

"She was not in the least embarrassed," pooh-poohed Chantal. "She was glad of the excuse to talk to him again, but Carlo made it plain to her that he did not believe in mixing business with pleasure, and rather ignored her. She was furious, especially after the amount of money she had spent on entertaining him, but there was nothing she could do about it, without making a complete fool of herself, was there?"

She turned from me to look teasingly at Peter.

"You know, I can quite understand why she found Carlo so attractive. He has that certain *'Je ne sais quoi'* which appeals to a woman, and of course he speaks near perfect English, and Betty Lawrence told me herself that it was nice to talk to a man in her own language after living in Milan for twelve years."

"But surely she talks to her husband in English!" I exclaimed.

"Apparently not. Since coming to live in this country, he has insisted on speaking in Italian. Of course, he is half-Italian, so it was easy enough for him."

"Lawrence does not sound an Italian name, and to me he looks a typical American."

"I expect he wants to have the best of both worlds," shrugged Chantal. "He was born in the States and lived there until he was thirty, but his mother was Italian, and her brother, who had no family of his own, invited his nephew to come to Milan to take charge of the family business some twelve years ago, and the way Mrs. Lawrence talked about it to me, he has turned this small business into a very thriving concern, and has no intention of ever returning to the States."

"What does Mrs. Lawrence feel about that?"

"As long as she has plenty of money to spend, and gets away from Milan occasionally, to enjoy the pleasures of Venice or Rome or Florence—

and I don't think she was meaning the museums and art galleries when she referred to pleasures—she raises no objection."

"Poor Lawrence! I wonder how he would feel if he knew how his wife was spending his hard-earned money?"

"I don't think you need waste any pity on Harry Lawrence," said Chantal coldly. "He and his wife are two of a kind. He has as keen an eye for a pretty girl as she has for the opposite sex!" She gave a shiver of distaste. "But there are ways and ways of being ogled at!"

I gathered that she did not like the way that Harry Lawrence had ogled her!

Chapter Eleven

THE SIGNS for the turn off for Peschiera and Desenzano showed up on the motorway, and we slowed down and turned off for the road to Lake Garda.

The countryside became more interesting, and I found myself paying more attention to the scenery than to Chantal's continuous flow of small talk.

We drove along tree-lined roads and past limpid pools and small streams and vineyards which stretched up the hill slopes.

Occasionally I caught a glimpse of a castle atop a hill, and then we came to the lake itself—deep and blue and shimmering in the morning heat haze. We drove along the lake side, past the long arm of land that points out into the water, with the castle of the Scaligers standing guard over the little township of Sirmione, famous since Roman times, which stand right at the tip of the promontory, with its ageless weeping willows, and the water, green with reeds, lapping its shore.

"We are going to Gardona Riviera," announced Peter. "It is about twenty minutes run from here. I know the proprietor of a small hotel there, which has its own private swimming beach, and we can have lunch and spend the day there if you like."

We drove on past Desenzano, with its crowds of tourists and its gay shops, along a straight, tree-lined road, and then for a time we lost sight of the lake as the road began to climb slowly inland, past more vineyards, and then as we topped the hill, there below us once more were the blue, blue waters of Garda, with lovely white villas set along its shore, half screened from our view by tall, straight cypresses which stood up, straight as sentinels on guard, and across the bay little townships clustered at the lake's edge, and others clung to the steep mountains which rose behind the lake.

We skirted Salò, where Mussolini centred his Fascist Government for a time during the Second World War, and drove along a busy, none-too-broad street, lined with pink and white and deep rose coloured oleander trees, and magnolias with great candlelike white blossoms, at which I kept exclaiming in pleasure, and then Peter turned sharp right into an entrance way between high stone walls, and continued down a steep, tree-lined drive, to draw up outside a large, ochre-coloured villa.

We received a friendly welcome from the proprietor of the hotel and his wife. Their son was one of the men Peter usually went climbing with in the Alps, and it was obvious that they thought a lot of Peter from the way they treated him.

The father opened up the cocktail bar specially for us, and insisted on standing us an

apéritif before our lunch, while his wife hurried
down to the kitchen, to tell the cook to prepare
Peter's favourite dish of rice in green peppers,
and to ensure that a table would be free for us
to dine whenever we wanted to.

We decided to have a swim before lunch, and
went out to the garden, where a porter was
busily erecting a great sun umbrella over a
round iron table only a couple of yards from the
stone parapet which separated the hotel garden
from the water of the lake.

We dumped our cameras and other parapher-
nalia on the table and went to change into our
swimming suits in the little wooden changing
rooms behind a hedge of oleanders.

There was a private jetty for boats in front of
the hotel, and this stone pier jutted out from
the tip of the crescent-shaped parapet, forming a
kind of breakwater.

From the parapet, a flight of steps led into the
water, which was waist deep at its shallowest
point, and while Peter and Chantal dived into
the lake from the end of the jetty and struck
out strongly for a wooden raft floating some distance out in the water, I contented myself by
climbing down the parapet steps into the lake,
which, after the warmth of the Lido, seemed ice
cold to begin with.

I swam the few yards from the parapet to the
end of the jetty, where I pulled myself up onto
the hot stonework, and sat down and watched
Peter and Chantal cavort around the raft, as at
home in the water as if it was their natural ele-
ment.

I wished I had been able to swim half as well as Chantal, because I felt rather left out of the fun, sitting on my own on the jetty. I gazed wistfully across the lake, to where a cypress-studded island seemed to float between sky and water in the pale blue haze of heat which hung over the lake.

The ferry steamer went past, crowded with tourists who leaned over the rails to watch the darting speedboats and the bobbing heads of the more daring swimmers who had ventured fairly far out into the lake.

I was fascinated by the bow-like figures of the water skiers who skimmed over the creamy wake of the motorboats which pulled them along.

One of the water skiers, in a black, rubbery-type suit, stirred a memory in my mind, but before I could place who he reminded me of, Peter pulled himself up onto the jetty beside me, shedding cold drops of moisture over my sun-warmed back as he brushed his dripping hair back from his forehead.

"How do you like it here?" he asked as he squatted down beside me, beads of lake water glistening like crystal on his forehead and square, sunburned shoulders.

"I much prefer the bathing here to that at Venice Lido," he continued. "It is never so crowded, and moreover you don't have to wade out for minutes before you are in deep water."

Chantal joined us, pulling off her white bathing cap and tossing her long fair hair free from its stricture.

"That was fun!" she smiled at Peter. "Much

better than getting hot and sweaty scrambling over the mountain tracks at Cortina!"

"I am glad you are enjoying yourself," he smiled back at her, "but I would enjoy myself more if you stopped flicking cold water from your hair down my spine!"

She grimaced at him, and gave a final annoying flick of her hair before leaving us, calling over her shoulder:

"I am going to change into a dry costume. I hate sunbathing in a wet one."

"It is about time we changed to go for lunch in any case," said Peter standing up and gazing towards the hotel, where already at the tables set out under the awning which shaded the terrace of the hotel the waiters were standing in readiness to serve the guests.

"What a pity your friend Ben Ferguson could not have come with us today," observed Chantal as Peter ordered our lunch. "This awful kidnapping will spoil your holiday for you, won't it, because I don't expect you will see very much of him as long as it is in the news."

She sighed. "It must be as trying for a woman to be married to a newsman as to a doctor," she said. "More so, perhaps, if he happens to be a globe-trotting newsman like your Ben. At least a doctor's wife has a settled home. No," she decided, as she twisted strands of spaghetti adroitly round her fork and popped it neatly into her mouth, "I might put up with a doctor's hours, but I should hate not to have a settled home."

This was my opportunity to repeat to Chantal

what I had tried to make clear to Peter, that Ben Ferguson and I were merely good friends, and that our stay in Venice had not been pre-arranged, but I was too busy trying to emulate Chantal's skilled manipulation of the long, thin strands of spaghetti to make a reply.

I could not get the hang of twisting the long, stringy pasta into a neat ball, and finally finished up by cutting it into manageable lengths with my fork and eating it, as Chantal teasingly informed me, in the true British fashion!

After lunch we lay in the sun for about an hour, before enjoying another swim, and then we went for a walk to the local shops, which overlooked the oleander-lined quayside.

Before we finally left on our return journey, Peter's friends in the hotel made iced coffee for us, and insisted that we sample their delicious chocolate gateau, a speciality of their cuisine.

Chantal decided she would like to sit in the back seat of the car for the return journey back to Venice. There she curled herself up like a contented cat, and by the time we reached the autostrada, she was sound asleep.

The change of air, the sunshine, a delightful sense of well-being and contentment combined to make me feel quite sleepy as well, but I did my best to keep awake and talk to Peter from time to time. However, the monotonous buzz of the tyres on the roadway combined with the monotonous scenery added to my lethargy and I too dozed off and did not waken until we stopped at the toll booth at the exit from the autostrada.

We drove from Mestre along the causeway to the garage where Peter's car was to be parked. The man in the office asked him if he had heard any more news about the kidnapped American girl, since the announcement that the kidnappers had demanded half a million dollars in ransom.

Peter told him that we had not even heard about the ransom demanded, and out of curiosity, on our way to the landing stage at the Piazzale Roma to catch the motoscafo for the Riva, he bought the latest edition of the *Corriere della Sera*, and opened it out to scan the front page.

I let out an astonished exclamation as I saw the photograph of Lauren Radcliffe, the kidnapped girl, which took up most of the space.

Surely this was the girl I had seen in the gondola which had glided past under my bedroom window the night Alice Sinclair had been murdered?

Chapter Twelve

"WHAT IS the matter, Melanie?" asked Peter sharply as he noticed my reaction.

"Peter, tell me, how long is it since that girl is said to have gone missing? Two nights?" I stared at him.

Peter nodded.

"She left her hotel suite the night before last, shortly after dinner, saying that she was going to meet a friend. Her father was talking to some business associates and did not pay much attention, neither asking who the friend was nor where she was going, and that was the last anyone seems to have seen of her."

I was still trying to persuade myself that I could be wrong in my identification. Young girls with thin faces, long blonde hair and characterless features do tend to look rather alike at first glance.

My gaze switched from Chantal, whose general description would tally with that of Lauren Radcliffe, to the picture in the paper, and I could see the dissimilarities. There was no use trying to deny the fact to myself.

The longer I stared at the photograph of the kidnap victim, the more certain I was that Lauren Radcliffe had been the girl I had seen in the gondola.

Reluctantly I spoke the words which were certain to involve me in the case.

"Peter, I saw this girl, the night before last, in a gondola which glided past under my bedroom window!"

Peter looked as startled as if he had been stung by a bee.

"Melanie, are you quite sure about this?"

I nodded slowly.

"Quite sure."

Chantal gaped at me, her big eyes registering her total surprise.

"Melanie! It couldn't have been!"

Peter had got over his initial amazement.

"If you are as certain as that, Melanie," he looked at me deliberately, "I think you should get in touch with Captain Cerutti the minute we get back to the hotel, and tell him what you saw. It could obviously be important."

I felt cold and shivery.

"Peter, I am sick to death of being involved with police and police investigations," I said feelingly. "Do you realise that this is the third time since I came to Venice a couple of days ago that this has happened?"

"But definitely the last!" said Chantal brightly, trying to cheer me up. "Things are supposed to go in threes, so at least you will know you have broken the spell after you talk to Captain Cerutti!"

Peter folded the paper, stuck it into his pocket and, taking a firm grip of my arm, hustled me towards the landing stage for the motoscafo.

Chantal followed close behind us, until we squeezed into the queue crowding into the vessel, and there we lost her in the crush.

Peter, as if he was afraid he might lose me too, kept a tight, reassuring clasp on my arm all the time we were pushing and shoving to get aboard, and somehow he managed to get a seat for me on the deck, between two well-laden housewives. He stood in front of me, like a prison guard, as if he thought I might still somehow elude him.

The women got out at the shopping place before S. Marco and Peter promptly sat down beside me before anyone else could occupy the space.

My hands had been nervously playing with the handle of my bag, and now he took one of them in his, as if he understood how nervous and annoyed and thoroughly fed up I was feeling, and wanted to comfort me.

I wondered if he would have made the gesture if Chantal had been with us, and if so what she would have said. I know if I had been in her place, I would have felt jealous of the action, but there was no sign of her at our side of the boat, and I was glad, because the warmth and strength of Peter's grip gave me the pleasantest of sensations, and for me, at least, it was all too soon time to get up and disembark for our hotel.

Peter did not even wait to see if Chantal had followed us off the boat as he hurried me down the gangway, and across the quay to the Capri, where he went immediately to the reception desk and asked the girl there to put through a call to Captain Cerutti at the Questura without delay.

At the urgency of his manner, a gleam of curiosity glinted in the girl's eyes, and she listened all ears to what he had to say when, after some delay, she managed to get the police captain on the line.

Peter, however, did not give her the satisfaction of finding out what his call was about. While I stood at his side, cold with nervous anticipation of the interview which lay ahead, he merely explained to Cerutti that there was something I had to tell him, which he felt required the captain's immediate attention, and that it would be wiser not to discuss the matter over the telephone.

There was a silence at the other end of the line for a second or two, and I could imagine that Cerutti was trying to determine just how important what I had to tell him was, and if it was worth his time to arrange to see me.

Peter must have been thinking the same thing, for before the captain replied, he said sharply:

"I can assure you, Captain Cerutti, that you will not be wasting your time if you see Signorina Lindsay straightaway. I would not have got in touch with you if the matter had been trifling."

I could hear Cerutti's voice in answer, and Peter said, "Right!" and replaced the receiver, just as Chantal looking disgruntled, came in through the swing doors.

"Where did you two get to?" she asked peevishly. "I didn't see you get off the motoscafo, and I was waiting for you at the landing stage. When there was still no sign of you after the boat left, I thought you must have got off at the wrong stage."

"We were first off," said Peter. "We didn't wait for you because I wanted to get on the 'phone to Cerutti without delay."

"Did you manage to get in touch with him? What did he say?" Chantal was all agog.

Peter gave her a warning look.

"We didn't want to broadcast why we are so anxious to get in touch with the police, Chantal," Peter told her, "so we did not say why we were calling, only that we had some information which we felt they might want to know straightaway."

"Didn't you even say that it was about—"

Peter interrupted her before she could say any more in front of the receptionist.

"Chantal, the same goes for you," he said firmly. "Please don't say a word of what we know to anyone."

"Or think we know!" Chantal added the rider. "After all, Melanie could have been mistaken."

"We shall soon know about that," said Peter, turning to me. "Cerutti wants you to go to the Questura right away."

"Oh!"

"I shall come with you," he smiled. "I know it is going to be a bit of an ordeal for you."

"Will you?" I gave him a grateful smile. "That will be wonderful."

Chantal shrugged.

"I hope you don't expect me to come too!" she said. "I suppose I should. A woman's company and all that. But Peter is much better at holding hands in comfort than I am. After all, it is a part of his profession, isn't it?"

"I must go up to my room to put on some fresh make up and tidy my hair," I said. "I need all the morale boosters I can think of!" I added with a shaky laugh.

"Don't be too long, Melanie," Peter warned me. "Cerutti said he was going to send a launch to fetch us on the instant, and the Questura is not far away. So hurry, please, we don't want to keep it waiting."

"Believe me, the sooner I get this interview over and done with, the happier I shall be, so that you don't need to tell me to hurry!" I snapped back, nerves adding an edge to my voice.

"Melanie, you have nothing to be nervous about," Peter noted the symptoms and tried to reassure me. "All you will have to do will be to make a statement, and then you will be free to come back here. After all, there is really not so very much you can tell them, is there?"

Somehow I had a premonition that the matter was not going to be quite as simple as Peter was making out, but as I walked towards the lift I tried to persuade myself that I was being unduly pessimistic.

I hurried to my room, hung up my damp bathing suit and towel, rinsed my hands and face with cold water to make me feel more wide awake and cool, hastily applied a touch of make up and returned to the foyer to rejoin Peter.

He was standing near the doorway talking to a smart young policeman whose grey uniform with its crimson piping and highly-polished black leather belt and pistol holster were being regarded with great interest by a freckle-faced English schoolboy who had arrived with his parents to stay at the Capri the previous evening.

The policeman saluted me as I approached, and then he led Peter and me out of the hotel to the police launch which was moored at the quay about fifty yards beyond the hotel.

Another policeman helped me to climb down into the launch. Peter and our accompanying officer jumped lightly down onto the deck, and almost at the same moment that their feet touched the boards, the motor of the craft roared to life, and we went speeding out from the quayside, causing the gondolas moored there to toss restlessly between their poles.

The vessel turned sharp right into a rio which debouched into the Canale di San Marco, passed under the arched bridge, and slowed down as it passed the leaning campanile of the Church of S. Giorgio dei Greci and continued along a small canal to the Questura, where it drew alongside a flight of steps.

Peter Somerville gave my hand a reassuring pressure as I mounted the flight of steps to the police station in the wake of the policeman who had come to the Capri to fetch us, and I gave him a tremulous smile of gratitude as we followed the young officer up another, inner flight of stairs, which led to a long corridor, which to my sensitive nostrils, smelt of damp and decay and disinfectant and stale tobacco fumes, and was totally depressing.

The man stopped outside a door in the corridor and gave a sharp knock before ushering us into a small, booklined office, where Captain Cerutti was seated behind a broad, dark wooden desk, his back to the window.

Captain Cerutti stood up as we came forward, and walked round the desk to shake hands with us.

"Signorina Lindsay, dottore—" he made a waving motion with his hand towards two moderately comfortable looking chairs drawn up to face the desk.

"*Prego, si accomodino,*" he murmured, and as we sat down, he leaned with his back against the desk, his hands resting on its sharp edge.

"*Bene.*" He looked from one to the other. "What is this so secret and important matter you wish to talk to me about?"

My mouth had gone dry and I had to lick my lips and swallow hard before I could summon my voice to reply.

"The girl who has been kidnapped—Lauren Radcliffe—I saw her the night before last!" The words came out with a rush.

Cerutti pushed himself away from the desk and straightened up as though a ramrod had been stuck down the back of his tightly-fitting jacket.

He stood over me, looking down at me with narrowed eyes.

"You are sure of this?" he snapped.

I nodded.

"Why did you not come to tell me about this sooner? We have been appealing all day for witnesses," he said angrily.

"I could not come forward earlier," I retorted, stung by his manner. "I had no reason to believe that the girl I had seen was the girl who had been abducted until little over an hour ago, when Peter, Dr. Somerville, bought a paper and I saw her photograph on the front page."

"Mmmph." Cerutti looked less displeased. "Tell me, then, where you saw this girl, and when, and if she was behaving normally." His eyes bored down into mine.

"I saw her in a gondola, which went past beneath the window of my hotel bedroom about, let me see—oh—I should say between one and two o'clock in the morning—the morning that Alice Sinclair was murdered."

"You saw her then?" Cerutti gave me a disbelieving look. "Are you quite sure?"

"Quite sure," I nodded in confirmation. "Yes, I am sure as can be that the girl was Lauren Radcliffe. I saw her plainly."

While Cerutti continued to look at me in disbelief, I added, "She had her eyes closed."

The police captain shook his head. "Signorina, this is a serious matter. Are you sure you are not imagining things? After all," he went on with deceptive mildness, "between one and two o'clock in the morning, surely the rio your window overlooks was very dark?"

"Indeed it was," I agreed. "At first I could not see the gondola, though I suspected the presence of some craft when I heard the movement of water below me when I was opening my window to let some cool night air into my room."

Cerutti opened his mouth to say something, but before the words could come I went on to explain hurriedly:

"That first night I was in Venice, I was unused to the heat and could not get to sleep. I had been advised not to open windows at night, but eventually I decided I simply must get some air, so—" I stopped short, "but of course you will know all this from the statement I have already given you of my actions the night Alice Sinclair was killed."

Cerutti snapped his fingers and gave a brisk order to the policeman who had accompanied us into the office. The man left the room, and Cerutti turned his attention to me once again.

"Until Goldoni returns with the file containing your statement, signorina, perhaps you would be good enough to go over the facts again."

I took a deep breath.

"Well," I began, "I opened the window for air, but fearing the possibility of mosquitoes, moths and the like, and knowing that if a light shone out into the darkness the insects would be immediately attracted towards it, I refrained from switching on any illumination. At that moment, all I could see was a blanket of dark, except for the silver of the skyline above the building opposite." I paused.

"Go on, signorina," encouraged Cerutti.

"I stood for a few seconds, enjoying the coolness of the night air, and heard these movements beneath the window. I glanced down, but there was nothing to be seen in the blackness, except an even deeper shadow, which seemed to move towards me. Just as I was about to turn away, the light in the room next to mine was switched on, and an area of the rio and the building opposite was lit up. It was as if a spotlight had suddenly been turned on. As I looked out once more, I heard Mrs. Sinclair open her window. Then she suddenly uttered an exclamation of surprise—"

"Do you think she had seen the people in the gondola?" asked Cerutti quickly.

"I expect she would, but I don't suppose she knew who the girl was, any more than I did, and she certainly did not stay at her window for more than a moment, because of the beetles which had upset her by flying in from the darkness. Remember, I told you that it was when she said, 'Darn these pesky beetles,' or words to that effect, that I realised who my next-door neighbour was?"

Cerutti looked at me intently. "Signorina, do you think the occupants of the gondola would have seen either you or Mrs. Sinclair?"

"I doubt if they could have seen me. My room was in darkness, and unless they had looked up before I spotted them, I don't think they could have seen Alice Sinclair, although they must have heard her exclamation. It was pretty explosive!"

Cerutti paced the floor, tapping his fingertips together as he did so, a thoughtful expression on his face.

"Signorina Lindsay, did the girl look up when the Signora Sinclair screamed?"

"She didn't exactly scream," I countered. "In any case, as I told you, when I saw her, the girl appeared to be asleep, and I didn't notice if Alice Sinclair's exclamation roused her. The gondola was only in my sight for seconds."

"How about the men who were with her? Did you have the opportunity to observe them?" Cerutti looked at me hopefully.

"I can't say I got a really good look at them. Mrs. Sinclair would have had a better view of them than I had, because the gondola had almost passed my window when her light went on."

"But did you see something of them?"

"There was one man close to the girl. All I saw of him was his back view, because when the light fell on the boat, he turned towards the girl, almost as if to shield her from its glare. At least, that is what I thought at the time." I gave a mirthless laugh. "I also thought they were lovers, from the way he acted towards her so protectively. If I had only realised—" my laugh became slightly hysterical, and Peter said gently:

"It is all right, Melanie. You are doing very well. Just take a deep breath. That will steady you up a bit." He smiled at me, a sweet, indeed a tender smile, which was as soothing as a tactual caress, and I managed to give him a shaky smile of gratitude in return, after I had followed his advice, and found that I had overcome the rising panic which had so unexpectedly assailed me.

I continued my story in a firmer tone.

"But I did catch a glimpse of the gondolier, Captain Cerutti. It was difficult to judge how tall he was, because I was looking down on him, but I got the impression he was of medium height. What really struck me as odd at the time was the way he was dressed. He was not wearing the usual gondolier outfit but had on one of those rubber black water-ski type suits with a black skull cap, or it could have been a rubber helmet, on his head."

"His face, signorina," interjected Cerutti impatiently. "Did you get a good look at his face? Would you know him again if you saw him?"

I tried to think back to the moment when I had looked down from my window on that memorable night. I had not paid particular attention to the man, and the moment of observation had been very fleeting.

I bit my lip in an effort to recall something more about him.

"I think he had rather fine features, a longish nose—" I shook my head. "It is difficult to describe him, because with the light shining down on him, from the angle from which it was coming, it had a rather distorting effect, possibly even elongating his features."

"Would you recognise him if you saw him again?"

I hesitated. I knew I was not being as helpful with my descriptions as Cerutti had been hoping, but I was doing my best, and not adding details of which I could not be sure.

"It is hard to say," I said at length. "Now when I think back to what he looked like, I have the vague feeling I could have seen him somewhere else, although I can't think where. But then," I shook my head, "I could be wrong about this. You must know only too well, in your profession, that a lot of people have similar characteristics, and could easily be mistaken for someone else."

"And there is nothing else you remember?" Cerutti tried to hide his disappointment.

I closed my eyes to try to recapture an elusive memory which had surfaced for the moment, and remembered something else.

"Yes. There was another thing I noticed about the gondolier. He had very thin, pale hands, and he wore a ring on his little finger. It must have been a fairly large ring for it to have caught my eye."

"On the little finger?" repeated Cerutti. "Of which hand?"

"The right one, I think. Yes, definitely the right one. He could have had rings on the fingers of his left hand, too, but I would not have seen them from the way he was holding the pole."

Cerutti nodded. "Good. Anything else? Could you make a guess at his age?"

"I am sorry. You must realise that I had only

a momentary glimpse of the gondola and its occupants, and until this moment I had not given
them another thought. Why, I did not even
realise I had noticed so much about them, until
you started asking me!" I shook my head. "No, I
could only make a very wild guess at his age.
But the other man, the one bending over the
girl, I would say," I hesitated, "yes, I would say
he was middle-aged. There was a heaviness
beneath the shoulder blades which you often get
in older men."

"And that is all you remember?"

"I am sorry I have not been able to help you
more."

"But you have been of invaluable help,
signorina!" Cerutti assured me with a courteous
smile. "Yours has been the only clear lead we
have had in the case. Now we know how the girl
was transported from her hotel. We know two
men at least are involved. We have some idea of
what they look like. You have nothing at all to
apologise for, Signorina Lindsay. In fact," he
gave me an odd look, "I am the one who is sorry
that you have become involved in police matters
yet again!"

"I am sorry about that, too, Captain Cerutti!"
I smiled at him, relieved that the interview was
almost over. "But I do wish I could have been of
much more help to you, so that you could lay
your hands on that poor girl's kidnappers
without further delay."

Goldoni, the policeman who had been sent to
get the file on the Sinclair case, returned to the
office as Cerutti was showing us out.

"Just leave the documents on my desk, Goldoni," said Cerutti, "then take the signorina and Dr. Somerville back to their hotel in the launch. On your way, ask Grego to come to my office."

The captain then turned to us and shook our hands.

"Thank you once again for your assistance, signorina." He looked at me. "There is one thing further I would ask of you. Please do not mention what you have told me this afternoon to anyone else, not even to your friend the Signore Ferguson. I do not want the press to get even a whiff of this information you have given me, do you understand?"

I nodded, although I could not help wondering why, when he trusted Ben with the story of the actual kidnapping, he was reluctant to have him know anything about the present, and to my mind, less important information I had given him.

I also wondered what the import was of the look which passed between Cerutti and Peter as I followed Goldoni from the room, but with so many other things to think about, I soon dismissed it from my thoughts.

Chapter Thirteen

CHANTAL WAS waiting for Peter and me in the foyer of the Hotel Capri.

As we came through the doorway, she came forward eagerly to meet us.

"Well?" she asked. "What did Cerutti say? Did he think it really was—"

"Chantal!" Peter interrupted her in a warning tone. "We have been asked not to say a word to anyone about the reason of Melanie's visit to him," he told her softly.

"But by now, everyone here knows that you and she had to go to the police station to see him!" objected Chantal. "They are bound to ask us questions, wanting to know what it was about."

"We shall just have to fob them off," Peter told her.

"But that won't be easy," she pointed out.

"We can always answer them with the time-honoured phrase that Miss Lindsay was helping the police with their inquiries, and let us hope they deduce from that that the inquiries were about the death of Mrs. Sinclair, which is feasible."

"But you will tell me what was said at the police station, won't you, Peter?" she smiled cajolingly up into his face. "After all, I know most of what Melanie had to tell them, so there won't be any harm in telling me that little more!"

She caught his arm and started to edge him towards the lounge.

"There is no one about just now, so you can speak here without being overheard."

I envied her the unselfconscious familiarity of her action as I turned from them to go to the desk to ask for the key of my room.

"There is a message for you, Signorina Lindsay," said the receptionist, fumbling for a note which had been stuck into the pigeon hole above my room number.

I took the note and glanced at it.

"The Signor Ferguson called and said he will come back to the hotel to meet the Signorina Lindsay at 20.00 hours this evening," read the message.

Good! I thought, and must have brightened visibly, because Peter, who, in spite of Chantal's blandishments, had followed me to the desk, asked curiously:

"Good news?"

I nodded.

"Ben is coming round to see me tonight at eight o'clock. I didn't think I would be seeing him today, considering what has been happening."

"Remember you have to say nothing to him about seeing Lauren Radcliffe," Peter repeated Cerutti's warning.

"Of course I'll remember," I said crossly. "All the same, I don't know why there should be all this secrecy about my seeing her, and I am quite sure Ben would not talk out of turn."

"He might act out of turn," said Peter oddly.

"What do you mean?"

"You know what newsmen are," he replied somewhat evasively. "He might try to do something on his own initiative, and get in the way of the police. Without meaning to, of course," he added hastily as he saw the expression on my face.

"In a way I am glad that I saw the kidnappers, because it does give the police a lead, doesn't it?" I said as I waited for the lift to descend. "I do hope they pick up these men soon, for poor Lauren Radcliffe's sake."

"I hope so, too!" said Peter with an amount of fervour in his voice that made me look round at him in surprise.

He was looking at me with a worried gleam in his eyes, a gleam that reminded me of the look he and Cerutti had exchanged in the police station.

"What is the matter?" I asked. "Don't you trust me to say nothing to Ben?"

Chantal, who had perforce to follow Peter to the lift instead of inveigling him to the lounge with her as she had wanted, gave me a sour look.

"It almost looks as if Peter doesn't even trust you out of his own sight!" she said in a sulky voice.

"Don't be an idiot, Chantal!" Peter rebuked her sharply. "Melanie has had enough to contend with today without you trying to be smart at her expense!"

"Oh!" Chantal drew in her breath with an exclamation of annoyance.

It seemed to me that an unnecessary tiff was about to develop between Chantal and Peter, and since I did not want to be responsible for a lover's quarrel, I interposed swiftly.

"You know, there is no need to worry about me. I am quite capable of looking after myself, Peter!" I turned my back on them and entered the lift.

As I was looking for the right button to press to take me to the first floor, I heard Peter mutter something in a low voice to Chantal, something which made her gasp, and thereafter I distinctly heard her say, "Of course!" and then, to my surprise, she and Peter stepped into the lift beside me.

"It's the second floor for you, isn't it, Peter?" I asked as my hand hovered over the lift button.

Chantal spoke up.

"Peter said you wouldn't mind showing me the window from which you spotted the kidnappers. Would you?" she begged hopefully.

"Why, no! Of course not!" I gave her a puzzled look. "You can come with me now, if you want."

"Mind if I tag along?" asked Peter when the lift stopped at the first floor.

"No! You come too by all means!" I invited him, although I was surprised by his request.

I could understand Chantal's curiosity to see what she would no doubt term "the scene of the crime," but what interest would it be to someone like Peter to come and stare down into a small, shadowy canal?

I unlocked the door of my room and stood aside for my guests to precede me into it.

"That is the window there, the one at the side," I told Chantal as I closed the door behind me, and followed her to the spot I had indicated.

She pulled aside the drapes, pushed the window further open and peered over the sill, down into the water.

"You must just have had the briefest glimpse of the gondola!" she said in a disappointed voice. "There could not have been a lot of light reflected out from a narrow window like this."

"It was from the light in Alice Sinclair's room that I saw them." I told my story yet again. "Since the side window is the main window in her room and takes up about half the wall space, there was quite a bit of light."

"Of course! I had forgotten that she was in the room next door to yours! Don't you feel at all upset at the thought?" Chantal craned her neck out of the window in an effort to see the adjoining apartment.

"There is no reason why I should be upset," I told her, watching her antics, and getting ready to grab her if she overbalanced, as she seemed in danger of doing.

Peter Somerville had not come to the window to see the view, but remained standing in the centre of the room, looking around him, seemingly more interested in the rococo decor than in the scene Chantal seemed to find so absorbing.

I looked across at him for a moment.

"At first, when I came into this room, I thought I had been given the bridal chamber by mistake!" I joked feebly.

"It does look splendid enough for that," he agreed with a smile.

Chantal claimed my attention again.

"I did not realise it was such a broad rio, but look, Melanie, there are two gondolas passing each other! One of them is laden with crates of vegetables and things. It seems to be stopping just past the window!"

She leaned out so far to see what was going on that I stepped forward and gripped the belt of her dress, a movement which only served to encourage her to lean out still further.

"Somehow I never thought of gondolas being used to deliver merchandise, did you? Look! They are unloading crates of Coca Cola now. How very unromantic! Coke and veg. instead of a lover and his lass and a singing gondolier! It seems all wrong somehow!"

As she was speaking, I heard a faint click behind me and as I glanced round to see what had caused the noise, I saw Peter moving away from the massive wardrobe.

Surely he hadn't been peering inside? The very idea was so inane, I almost giggled.

As I watched him, he bent down by the side of the bed, and proceeded to tie up his shoe lace, which explained the sound I had heard in a more satisfactory manner, for now I deduced that it had been the noise of the metal lace tab knocking against the leather upper of his shoe.

He straightened up and looked across at the window.

"Surely you have seen all you want to see by this time, Chantal?" he asked. "I think it is time we left Melanie in peace to get dressed for her evening date."

Chantal reluctantly withdrew from the window.

"Ben is lucky to have time off tonight," she told me. "I am quite sure poor Carlo will still be on duty."

"Or perhaps he is having an apéritif with Mrs. Lawrence in her now hotel!" suggested Peter wickedly, giving me a wink as if he was amused, rather than annoyed at her interest in the young Italian.

"You don't really think that!" Chantal looked crestfallen. "Oh! You are just trying to tease me!" she added as she caught the tail end of the wink. "Just because you couldn't make a date for tonight, there is no need to—"

"But if Carlo isn't free, surely I have a date with you for tonight?" Peter interrupted her blandly. "And what could be nicer than that?"

He took her by the arm.

"Come on, my dear. It is time you went to dress for dinner. You know how long that usually takes you!"

After they had gone, I went over to shut the side window, which Chantal had left open. The gondola at the kitchen entrance of the hotel was still unloading its cargo and I stood idly watching it. The man carrying the crates of vegetables up the slippery steps glanced up, and seeing me watching him, he gave me a leering smile.

I promptly retreated, shutting the window with a forceful bang, and pulling the curtains across it.

Chantal may have needed an hour and a half to dress for dinner, but I did not, and I wondered how I could fill in the time before Ben's arrival at eight o'clock.

I was so glad that he could come tonight. Dear Ben, it was no wonder I loved him, I smiled to myself. He had always been such a good friend to me since I was a youngster, treating me in a casual affectionate way as one of the family, chivvying me out of bouts of self pity when adolescent love affairs went wrong, always having the knack of somehow setting my world to rights. He was favourite uncle, big brother, schoolgirl idol rolled into one truly dependable friend. If I had wanted, he would have let me cry on his shoulder without embarrassment, although tonight, when I was almost in the mood for such a cry, I could not have made use of him, or he would have wondered what was up, and because of my promise to Cerutti, I could not have explained that for some reason I felt edgy and uneasy, and, yes almost frightened!

I prowled restlessly round the room, wondering what to do with myself for the next hour or so.

I picked up the thriller I had bought on my outward journey to Venice, and tried to read, but I could not concentrate on the plot, and after struggling through a few chapters, I put the book down again, and went to stand on the little balcony of my front window.

Late afternoon was turning with surprising haste to evening. Ships and islands stood out in unnatural relief against the molten glow of the sky as the sun prepared for its setting.

Underneath my window, someone laughed, and my heart rose to my throat, almost strangling my breath as I recognised that laugh—a deep, infectious sound.

I peered down over the railing of the balcony.

Peter Somerville was standing almost directly below me, talking to the freckle-faced schoolboy and his father.

I could not see Peter's face, but as he stood there, legs slightly astride, thumbs tucked into his trouser pockets, as he talked in a manner which had become familiar to me in the past two days, I did not have to see his face to guess at its expression.

His attractive eyes, one slightly drawn down in the corner by the threadlike line of an old scar which ran from brow to brow, would be glinting. There would be a network of laughter wrinkles radiating from the corners of his eyes and mouth, and if he had not yet had his usual pre-dinner shave, there would be a dark shadow down his cheeks and round his strong chin.

A youngish woman joined the group beneath my balcony and I heard the Englishman introduce her to Peter as his wife.

Peter held out his hand to her in acknowledgement of the introduction, and his hand touched hers. I closed my eyes, imagining the firmness of his grip, and again, almost physically, I recalled the strength and comfort of his hand as it had held mine that afternoon on the journey in the motoscafo from the Piazzale Roma to the hotel, and I quivered with the remembered pleasure.

It was at that moment that I realised that while I dearly loved Ben Ferguson, as one dearly loves a member of one's own family, I had fallen in love, suddenly, unreasonably, and quite, quite hopelessly, with Dr. Peter Somerville.

Chapter Fourteen

I STOOD gripping the rail of the balcony and tried to tell myself that the very idea was insane. Quite, quite insane!

In spite of the books I had read, the love ballads I had listened to, the romantic notions I had had as an adolescent, in real life, things like this did not happen. There was no such thing as love at first sight.

"I am being utterly ridiculous!" I spoke the words aloud in my effort to deny it.

Peter must have heard the sound of my voice, for as he was walking from the family to whom he had been speaking, he stopped and looked up at the balcony.

Our eyes met. Once again I experienced that weak-kneed, breathless feeling which an unexpected look from him could induce, and a slow flush burned my cheeks, making them match the reflected light of the setting sun on the mellow pink walls of the hotel.

"Hello, there!" he called up, smiling. "Haven't you changed for dinner yet? You are not leaving yourself very much time."

"Ben is never on time for a date." I was surprised how normal my voice sounded in spite of my inward shakiness. "And I hate to hang about when I am all dressed up."

"Why not join Chantal and me in the cocktail bar until Ferguson arrives?" suggested Peter. "She said she would be ready in about another half an hour."

I was torn between the bitter-sweet desire to be with Peter, and the saner knowledge that the way I was feeling, I would be wise to avoid him as much as possible.

Desire won.

"If Chantal doesn't mind, I should be delighted to join you," I replied.

"Good!"

I persuaded myself that he sounded genuinely, and not merely politely pleased at my acceptance.

"I shall see you in half an hour," he added. "Till then!" With a wave of his hand he turned and continued on his way to the edge of the quay.

I went back into my bedroom, my feelings alternating between delight and dolour as I dressed with impatient haste for my rendezvous at the cocktail bar.

To my disappointment, Peter had not yet arrived in the little bar when I went downstairs, and I wondered whether to wait there on my own and order an aranciata, or go for a stroll along the Riva to admire the fascinating display of lights which illumined the quayside, outlined the great liner anchored off the Danieli, flooded the Paladian church on San Giorgio, and danced and shimmered with magic lantern effects on the waters of the lagoon.

A couple of young men at the bar counter eyed me up and down, making no effort to conceal their interest in a lone female, and I decided to beat a retreat.

However, I had not even reached the doorway when Ben, early for a date for the first time since I had known him, came hurrying into the hotel.

"Melanie!" he exclaimed in surprise. "I thought that I was going to be early for a change!"

"You are!" I assured him with a smile, adding, "It just happens that I am very early, too!"

He laughed.

"I am glad of that. It gives us all the more time together. Where do you want to go tonight? Harry's Bar again, or Quadri's? Or have you some other place in mind?"

"I hadn't thought." I hesitated. "Shall we have a drink here first while I make up my mind?"

"Surely!" He led the way back to the cocktail bar, greeted his friend Pino who was serving there, and climbed onto the bar stool beside mine.

"What did you do with yourself today, Melanie?" he inquired. "A tour of the Doge's Palace, the Bridge of Sighs, the Campanile, or what?"

"Believe it or not, Ben, I haven't started sight-seeing as yet. Having come to Venice to do just that, I spend one afternoon bathing on the

Lido, and the next day driving away from the city to enjoy the delights of bathing at Gardone Riviera!"

He eyed me shrewdly.

"With your young doctor friend."

"He is not my young doctor!" I replied with undue sharpness.

Ben's eyes narrowed. "No, he isn't, is he? He came to Venice with that very pretty little blonde, didn't he?" He looked round as if he was hoping to get another glimpse of Chantal's charms, and was disappointed because she wasn't there. "Are they engaged?"

I felt my cheeks would crack with my effort to keep on smiling.

"I would not know. She certainly does not wear an engagement ring, and she does not spend all her time with Peter, either, for that matter. She spent last night flirting with Captain Cerutti's right-hand man—the dark, good-looking one—Carlo somebody or other. They went for a ride in a gondola."

Ben frowned. "That was not very wise. Carlo has the reputation of being a bit of a Don Giovanni. I hope she knows how to handle him."

"She seems to. She evidently insisted that his friend went too, and I think they all intended to go swimming at the Lido today, only Carlo was recalled to duty because of the kidnapping."

"Doesn't Somerville object?" Ben was surprised. "I most certainly would not let my girl gad around with a handsome Italian if we were on holiday together."

"Ben! You would never have time to go on

holiday with a girl!" I teased him. "Do you know, I shall feel very sorry for your wife, when you marry—if you ever manage to find time to do that!"

He shrugged. "The girl I marry will have to accept my way of life too!" he replied.

He raised his glass to mine.

"Let's drink to love!"

I sipped at my drink, while my eyes kept straying towards the door, wondering how soon Peter would arrive.

"By the way, Melanie," Ben swung his stool round to face the door too. "Remember I said I thought I had either seen or heard something about Somerville before?"

I nodded.

"I was on the 'phone to London today and I asked Joe Harrison—remember him?—if he could find out about him for me."

"Ben!" I expostulated.

He looked at me unsmiling.

"I do not like being puzzled about people, especially attractive men who take an interest in my best girl!"

"Really, Ben!" I felt a flush of annoyance stain my cheeks. "Peter Somerville does not take a special interest in me!"

"No?" Ben raised his eyebrows. "You have been here a mere two days, and already you have been out with him twice. Wouldn't you say that that was a special interest?"

"He was merely being kind. He knew how upset I was by the murder of Mrs. Sinclair, and knowing I was on my own, he thought I might be in need of company."

"His interest did not seem like mere sympathy to me," said Ben firmly, "especially when he had a perfectly good girl of his own, so in your interests, I thought I should learn more about him."

"And?" My curiosity overcame my annoyance.

"He is quite a lad, this Dr. Somerville. He works in London's dockland, where he also runs a club for old people. He is well liked, and when he isn't taken up with his profession, he climbs mountains."

"I knew about that!"

"Did you, now? And did you also know that he is quite famous as a mountaineer?"

I shook my head in surprise.

"Oh, yes! I knew I had seen his face before, and that I hadn't associated him with the medical profession. The moment Harrison mentioned mountaineering, I remembered I had seen his photograph, among a party of men who climbed the North Face of the Eiger last year!"

"Oh!" I was taking in everything Ben was telling me about Peter with maximum interest. "He did tell me that he enjoyed climbing and winter sports, and that he would have been climbing in the Alps again this year if it hadn't been for Chantal, but I did not realise he was a famous mountaineer."

"Chantal must have quite a hold over him, to make him forgo his favourite recreation, and then flaunt her power by flirting with other

young men in his presence. Poor man!" he said
with a degree of sympathy. "Perhaps he asks
you out to show her that two can play at that
game, but I would rather he flirted with some
other girl!"

I did not like Ben's insinuation that Peter
was making use of me to get his own back on
Chantal.

I hurriedly gulped down the rest of my drink
and was going to suggest to Ben that it was time
we leave the Capri and go on to Quadri's, when
Carlo Benvenuto came into the bar and sat
down beside us.

"Buona sera, signorina, signore," he greeted
us.

Ben returned the greeting, and from the
speculative look in his eyes, I realised that we
were not going to leave just yet. Carlo was a
policeman, involved in the kidnapping case Ben
was writing about, and he might be able to give
Ben some more information about it.

"What do you wish to drink?" he asked Carlo,
signalling to Pino.

There followed a polite argument as to who
would order for whom. Ben won, and I was
trapped unwillingly for the duration of another
round.

"Any more news from headquarters?" Ben
asked Carlo the inevitable question. "Is Radcliffe going to pay the ransom demanded, or has
he changed his mind?"

"He is going to pay, naturally!" Carlo's brows
lifted. "No father could refuse to do so, when his
daughter's life is the price."

"If she is still alive!" said Ben grimly.

"Naturally Radcliffe has made one stipulation before he hands over the money," said Carlo. "He wants proof that his daughter is alive and unharmed, and if he gets this proof he is willing to hand over the ransom money within forty-eight hours."

"Why forty-eight hours?" I asked. "Is that to give the police time to trace the men?"

"It is to give Radcliffe time to lay his hands on that much money!" said Ben. "Half a million dollars is not the kind of money you have lying around, ready to be uplifted at a moment's notice."

"Half a million! He must be tremendously rich!"

"He won't be after this! It means he has to sell off all his assets in America to get the cash, and it also means goodbye to the hopes he had of taking over the firm in Italy—the transaction which brought him to Venice in the first place."

"Goodbye to his daughter, too!"

Peter who had come up behind us unobserved made the declaration in a grim voice. "How many cases have you heard of, Ferguson, where the victim is returned alive?"

"But surely if the money is paid, the kidnappers must keep their side of the bargain!" protested Chantal, as Carlo offered her his seat.

"And not be able to enjoy spending the money?" Peter shook his head. "I doubt it. The girl is bound to have seen or heard something during her captivity, which could lead to their capture. Do you think that they are going to take that risk?"

"Ben, you don't think they will kill her, do you?" I asked, willing my eyes away from Peter.

"Kidnapping is a major crime, Melanie," he replied slowly. "People who stoop to such a method to obtain money have no moral scruples. If they think they will be caught, because there is a witness to testify against them, then I don't think murder would be beyond them."

"Oh, no!" gasped Chantal, and under her golden tan her cheeks paled. "Peter!" She turned to Somerville. "Do you honestly think they would kill for that reason?"

I could not help turning to look at Peter myself.

There was a strained look in his eyes, and his mouth was shut in a tight, uncompromising line.

"There is always hope, Signorina Chantal," Carlo intruded in the conversation. "As a man who deals daily with criminals, I should know, yes? No, no!" he went on with a shake of his head to emphasise the point. "I believe the signorina will be released to her father when the money is paid over, and that already her kidnappers have their escape route planned to South America or some such place where our law cannot catch up with them."

"Yes!" Chantal turned to him with relief flooding her face. "You should know more about criminals than we do! Oh! I hope Lauren's father gets the money quickly and then we shall all be put out of suspense."

Ben's attention focussed back to Carlo.

"Are you not on duty tonight, Signor Benvenuto?" he asked. "I thought Captain Cerutti said he would be working twenty-four hours a day on this case, and his men, too?"

Carlo shrugged.

"I have been granted sick leave signore. A sick man cannot give of his best, as even Captain Cerutti recognises."

"You don't look ill to me, Carlo!" Chantal inspected him with her wide-eyed gaze. "What do you say, Peter?"

"I doubt if Signor Benvenuto would have been granted sick leave at this particular moment if he was as well as he looks," he replied.

There was a harshness in his voice which I had not heard before, and looking at him again covertly from under my eyelashes, I realised he was far from being in a good humour. I wondered how much Chantal's behaviour had to do with this, because once again she was ignoring Peter and had switched her full attention to Carlo, asking him how long he expected to be off duty, and if he was too ill to go swimming with her at the Lido on the following morning.

"You know," she glanced at me, "Carlo is a perfect wizard on water skis. I was watching him perform one day last week." She turned to him. "You were certainly not ill then! Even Peter said you were so good he would not mind taking a lesson from you!"

I could not bear to watch the unchangingly grim expression on Peter's face, so I finished my drink, slipped off the bar stool and announced:

"Ben and I are going to Quadri's now."

"So you have made up your mind at last!" Ben drained his glass and put it down on the counter. "I hope we manage to get a table."

"I love Quadri's!" I heard Chantal say to Peter as we were leaving. "Couldn't we go there, too?"

I also heard Peter's firm "No" as Ben ushered me through the glass doors and out into the night, and although minutes earlier I had wanted to get away from his presence, I felt cast down by his reply.

Chapter Fifteen

BEN AND I strolled arm-in-arm along the Riva, neither of us speaking, because Ben never does indulge in small talk, and I was preoccupied, thinking about Peter.

The night air was warm and unusually still, and there were many other evening strollers ambling, like us, in the direction of the Piazzetta.

Light spilled across the Riva from the doorways and windows and danced on the black wavelets of the Canal. Music from the transistor of a couple we were passing whispered a love song into the air.

"Love for love," murmured the singer's voice.

Love for love, how wonderful that must be, I thought, and sighed.

"Something troubling you, Melanie?" Ben looked down at me.

"I was thinking that this must be the most romantic city in the world!" I answered his question.

"Don't let Venice go to your head, my dear!" he warned me. "Enjoy its beauty, its buildings, its paintings, its shops, its history, and even the sense of being in a fairyland that it gives you, but don't let it make you vulnerable to romance."

He gave my arm an affectionate squeeze.

"I am glad I am here with you to keep an eye on you and help fend off the two-legged wolves who abound here. I didn't like the way young Carlo was watching you tonight, or Somerville either for that matter! In fact, my dear, you are too damned attractive to be wandering around strange cities on your own, and if you will take advice from an elder," he chuckled, "I'll not say a better, please keep to the beaten tracks, don't go wandering down dark alleys on your own, and Venice abounds in dark alleys—and preferably go out in a foursome rather than tête-à-têtes with handsome young men, present company excluded, of course!"

"Dear Ben!" I smiled at him. "I am a big girl now! Sometimes I don't think you realise that I have grown up. Although I still dream dreams, I keep my eyes open, and I am very well able to look after myself, only—"

"Only?" he echoed.

"Only it is very nice to have you around on occasion too!" I returned his affectionate squeeze.

We had crossed the Ponte della Paglia to the Mole and had reached the lagoon side of the Piazzetta, where stand the two great Oriental granite columns set up there in the twelfth century, the one with the Assyrian lion, the symbol of St. Mark poised atop, and the other with the statue of St. Theodore, the patron saint of Venice, on a crocodile.

Ben stopped between the columns.

"Melanie, did you know that in the good old

days, this was the spot where they erected a scaffold with a black cross and a wooden block, to cut off the heads of the wrongdoers? Even today, when a Venetian says you are between St. Mark and St. Theodore, he means you are in a most unenviable position!"

"I hope no one ever says that to me!" I gave a quick shiver. "Come on, Ben!" I urged him forward. "Let us not tempt fate by standing here any longer!"

He laughed.

"One minute you tell me that you are a sensible young woman, well able to take care of herself, and the next, you let a superstitious story upset you!"

I shrugged uneasily. "I seem to be susceptible to atmosphere, Ben, and there is something in the air tonight that makes me feel uneasy."

"There is probably a storm brewing out over the Adriatic. It is hot and still enough for one of the spectacular electric storms you sometimes get here, and conditions like these can upset the nerves." He found an answer for my mood.

"Or perhaps I am just plain hungry!" I tried to laugh off my uneasy feeling. "I have had nothing to eat since one o'clock, and these orange drinks I had in the bar have gone to my head!"

We crossed to the arcade, where balls of light hung from each arch and cascaded their brilliance across the slabs of the Piazza.

"How about an apéritif in Florian's before we go across to Quadri's?" suggested Ben. "We might as well make an evening of it. I don't know when I shall be free again to squire your around."

"Ben!" I protested, "you mustn't feel that you have to spend all your spare time with me! You must have other friends here you want to see."

"I can see them any time," he replied. "It isn't often I can get so much of your company," he went on amiably, "and in any case, I haven't caught up with all the news from home yet!"

He took my elbow and guided me towards a table on the perimeter of the rows spilling from the arcade out into the Piazza itself, which a couple had just vacated.

We reached it only seconds ahead of a quartet of American sailors, who disconsolately went back out into the square to await for another opportunity to get a table.

"That was lucky!" said Ben, signalling to the waiter who was hovering nearby, and ordering two Camparis and soda.

"Now, tell me, while I remember to ask, what happened to the Manor House in the village? Was it turned into a roadhouse, or was it taken down?"

For a quarter of an hour or so we chatted of the affairs of our home town in Angus, and for the first time for hours I began to feel relaxed and forget all about my present worries.

Alice Sinclair, the murderous bag snatcher, the men who had kidnapped Lauren Radcliffe seemed to be mere figures in an old nightmare, fleeting and insubstantial as a bad dream, as

Ben and I talked happily of the normal world of our mutual background.

I had just finished my Campari, and Ben was trying to catch the waiter's eye to get the bill for our drinks, when an unexpected, eardrum deafening noise made me push my chair back with a start.

Ben grinned. "It is only the Bronze Moors on the Clock Tower performing their hourly ritual," he told me. "Surely you have heard them do their bludgeoning act before?"

I nodded. "Yes, on my first day here. But they seem to make so much more noise at night!" I made myself heard between the strokes which reverberated in my ears as though the noise they caused was pressed down onto the square by the weight of the night's darkness.

Even the pigeons, which surely should have accustomed themselves to the noise by this time, went swirling around and around until it was over, and they could settle once more and smooth their ruffled feathers.

"We are just in nice time for dinner." Ben stood up. "I don't think we should have too much trouble getting a table at Quadri's. I know the head waiter."

"You make a habit of knowing the right people, don't you?" I teased him.

"In my profession, knowing the right people at the right time is an invaluable asset," he replied lightly, as he helped me on with my duster coat.

A light drizzle had begun to fall, and the damp slabs of Istrian stone reflected back the lights from the arcades as we hurried across to the other side of the Piazza and passed under the curved arch which led to Quadri's.

We went upstairs, where a waiter conducted us to a table beside an open window overlooking the Piazza.

We were both handed menus, but as at Harry's Bar, I invited Ben to choose for me, while I stared with interest round the pleasant, softly-lighted room in which we were seated, and then out at the Square, to the lighted colonnade on the other side, and the table which we had vacated there, and which the American sailors were now occupying.

The rain was getting heavier, and people were hurriedly leaving the tables which were in the open and moving under the arcade for shelter. I could hear the ominous rumble of thunder as the storm drew nearer, and for the twinkling of an eye, the lights in the restaurant and the Square flickered as a vivid display of lightning zig-zagged across the sky, outlining the domes of St. Mark's and the topmost turret of the Campanile, and seeming to linger over the Procuratie.

The rain was now beating so heavily against the pavement of the Piazza that it sounded like a perpetual fusillade of shot.

"How long will this go on for?" I asked Ben as I continued to stare with fascination at the enlarging puddles on the ground below.

"Quarter of an hour, half an hour, or half the night!" He shrugged. "And since this is Venice,

I shan't even be able to hail a taxi to get you back to your hotel dry!"

"If this keeps up, at the rate the pools are spreading, we shall be able to take a gondola from door to door!" I smiled as I watched the antics of two elegantly-dressed young women who were making a dash across the Square to the shelter of the arcade on the opposite side.

There was a group of people standing under cover of the arch where the girls were trying to push their way in, and at first they would make no move to let the girls past, but then one of the men moved to one side, and turned round to have another look at the two attractive women as they pushed past him. Something about this movement, as much as his build, reminded me of the man who had been seated beside Lauren Radcliffe in the gondola.

I started forward in my chair, and strained my eyes to look at him when he turned back again to face the Square, but his features were indistinct in the shadow of the colonnade, and his face a mere blob of white which, even had I been able to see it, would have meant nothing to me. He continued to stand there, long after those around him had found seats at the tables, or moved on, and for no good reason, he made me begin to feel uneasy once more.

I was glad when the waiter came across to close the window beside me, and shut out the sounds of the storm, the occasional spray whipped onto the table by a gust of wind over the sill, and the sight of that man, standing alone, looking across at the entrance of Quadri's, as though he was waiting for someone to enter or emerge from the restaurant.

However, I soon forgot all about him as the meal progressed, for Ben had chosen the menu with care.

Thin slices of prosciutto with black olives were the forerunners of the main course of suckling pig stuffed with herbs and truffles, a dish which I had never tasted before, and which was more delicious than I could have imagined it to be. I enjoyed each morsel of it, and each mouthful of the Valpolicello which Ben had ordered to be drunk with it.

For dessert there was a cloud light zabaglione, followed by coffee, strong and black, with thick cream floating on the surface, and Courvoisier to evoke a mood of mellowness, and with the soft lights, the good food and Ben's undemanding company, I felt contented as a pampered cat, and ignored the crashing of the thunder which from time to time drowned out the steady splash of the torrential rain, and the vivid flashes of lightning which seared the sky.

I was also happily unaware that the man who had caused my moment of unease still stood in the archway opposite, his back against a pillar, staring at the doorway of Quadri's, waiting for me to make my exit.

Chapter Sixteen

At ten o'clock it was still raining as heavily as ever, and the rain showed no sign of letting up, although the thunder was growling less ominously, and there were longer intervals between its rumblings.

Ben kept looking at his watch and at length decided that rain or no rain we would have to leave the restaurant.

"I ought to be able to borrow an umbrella from one of the staff," he told me hopefully, "but I am afraid that your feet are going to be soaked by the time we get back to the Capri."

I glanced down at my elegant, black patent shoes, which I knew would never be the same again after the proposed wade across the Piazza, and decided that whatever Ben's reaction, I was going to remove them and walk back to the hotel barefoot.

We made our way down the stairs and, before we could spot our waiter with his umbrella, there, standing in the doorway, the rain still dripping from his crisp black hair and plastic raincoat, we saw Peter Somerville.

He smiled with relief when he saw us.

"I was hoping I hadn't missed you!" He

stepped forward as he spoke and handed me a parcel which he took from under his raincoat.

"I asked the chambermaid to go to your room and fetch me your waterproof and bathing shoes, the only answer I could think of to the question of what shoes you could walk home in!" He smiled at me and then turned to Ben.

"I also managed to borrow an umbrella from the hotel porter for you. Sorry I could not manage anything else."

"Peter! How very thoughtful of you!" I gave him a most grateful smile. "Wasn't it?" I turned to Ben.

He was looking at Peter with a curious, almost calculating look in his eyes, and Peter was regarding him in much the same way, almost, I thought ridiculously, as if they were a couple of fighting cocks weighing each other up.

As I changed my shoes, I heard Peter say to Ben:

"I think you should know about the special news flash which came over the radio about half an hour ago."

He looked from Ben down to where I was kneeling, pulling on the bathing shoes.

"The police have announced officially that they have a witness to the kidnapping; someone they say who can identify the kidnappers, and so they are urging the men in question to give up their prisoner now, before they are caught, and so face a lesser sentence than they might if they continue with their ransom demands."

Ben tensed.

"I heard a rumour to the effect that such a

witness had turned up, but there are always rumours at a time like this, and most of them time-wasting. I suppose the police were trying to keep this under their hats as long as possible because—"

"Because they did not want Melanie to become the centre of attraction for the second time," said Peter, looking Ben in the eye.

"Cerutti said we were to say nothing to you," he went on rapidly, "but now that the story has been released, I doubt if you would have found difficulty in discovering who the witness was, and for the sake of your friendship with Melanie, in spite of Cerutti's warning, I think you should know all the facts."

Ben let out a long whistle of breath.

"Thank you, Somerville." He returned Peter's steady gaze. "It is not a very pretty kettle of fish, is it?"

I stood up. "Ben, you must think it awful of me to say nothing, when we are such good friends, but Cerutti was very firm about not telling you. He wanted as few people as possible to know there was what he called a key witness."

"You can understand his reasoning, can't you, Ferguson?"

Ben's face was grim. "Naturally I understand!" He glanced at me. "What I cannot understand is how he could let me take Melanie out tonight!"

"Cerutti strikes me as a very able man. I know he feels he has taken the necessary precautions." Peter gave a slight jerk of his head, as if to reassure Ben. "And now, don't you think we should be getting back to the hotel as quickly as possible? There are more comfortable places to linger in than this gloomy doorway."

Ben put up the umbrella Peter had brought for him, and took me by one arm, while Peter took the other, and they both held me so tightly I felt I must look as if I was under police escort. Even their faces looked grim as gaolers' as they hustled me through the rain and the shadows across the square and down the Piazzetta towards the quay, but whereas Ben's grip was stolid and vice-like, Peter's though equally firm, had a certain tenderness. Or was this mere hopeful imagination on my part?

We were not the only ones abroad in the rain that night. A group of young men were larking in our wake, and as we came under the lights of the arcade, I spotted a couple of carabinieri sheltering from the downpour beside one of the pillars, and there was another policeman standing near the Ponte della Paglia as we approached the bridge.

I was glad to get back into the hotel. In spite of the shelter from the umbrella Ben had been holding, there were raindrops on my face, and the ends of my hair trailed dankly on my shoulders. My feet squelched inside the bathing shoes, which looked out of place with the rest of my sophisticated get-up, and I did not linger with Ben and Peter, who had suggested a nightcap in the bar.

Instead, I went directly to my room to strip

off my damp clothes and enjoy the comfort of a piping hot bath.

I was glad Ben had not been angry with me for not telling him about my visit to the Questura in the afternoon, but of course he would appreciate my reasons for not doing so. Probably he and Peter were discussing the whole unfortunate business at this very moment, while they sipped the last drink of the day.

As I crept into bed, I could hear someone moving about in the room next to mine. Murder or no murder, there is always such a shortage of accommodation in Venice during the tourist season, no room remains vacant for long, and I was rather glad in a way to know that there was someone so close to hand.

Next morning Venice was the Venice of Canaletto. There were turquoise skies with their deeper reflections in the lagoon. Rose pink and cream and white buildings and palaces, washed by the overnight rain, sparkled in the early morning sunlight, and there was not a whisper of cloud in the sky as evidence of the previous night's storm.

Today, I decided, as I dressed myself, would be an ideal day for seeing the lovely palaces, the romantic bridges, the glorious paintings and the churches for which Venice is rightly famed, so I armed myself with a guide book and a map, and went down to breakfast, determined to start my expedition as early as possible.

Peter was sitting at a table on his own, and

when he saw me, he stood up, smiling, and invited me to join him.

"Where is Chantal this morning?" I asked him. "Has she slept in?"

"She has gone off with Carlo to see if she can get an English newspaper."

"Carlo must surely have called for her very early!" I expressed my surprise.

Peter shrugged. "He says he intends to make the most of his sick leave!"

"And you don't mind?" I frowned as I buttered a roll with more than usual care.

"Why should I?" Peter countered. "Marguerita—my sister—asked me to keep an eye on Chantal, but I don't think that was intended to mean that I was to play the part of, well, what do you call a male duenna?" he chuckled.

"I—I don't understand!" I stuttered. "You don't mean to say that Chantal is your niece?" I shook my head incredulously. "She can't be!"

Peter grinned. "Why ever not?"

"I—I don't know!" I looked at him and kept on looking at him and tried not to smile too delightedly with the sheer relief of knowing what his relationship to the pretty blonde he was squiring around was.

"My sister is twelve years older than I am," Peter went on to explain. "She was married at the same age that Chantal herself is now. She and her husband live very near to me in London, and we see a lot of each other.

"Chantal and my sister had planned this holiday in Venice for months, as a special coming-of-age present for Chantal, whose eighteenth birthday was a few days ago.

"The rooms in the Capri and the flight were booked before Christmas, and then," he smiled, "you know what they say about the best laid plans! To everyone's surprise and to everyone's delight, too, Marguerita became pregnant again. The baby is due in three months' time, but because of her age and general condition, my sister's doctor advised her, only three weeks ago, to cancel her trip!"

"Oh, no!" I cried.

"Her parents did not want Chantal to come here on her own, and her friends could not afford to come with her, and poor Chantal was very upset. She is at the age when temperament rockets to heaven or plumbs the depths—but you will have been at that stage much more recently than me, so you will understand!" His eyes twinkled.

"At any rate, she became so depressed, and her mother worried so, that for everybody's sake, I said that since I had happened to arrange my holiday for the same time, instead of going to Switzerland, I would come to Venice with Chantal. After all, the Alps will be there for another year, but a girl is only eighteen once—or should be!" he added lightly.

"How kind of you to sacrifice your holiday like that."

"Kind of me?" He was surprised. "Anyone in my position would have done the same thing. That is what a family is for, isn't it?"

I stirred sugar into my coffee and stared down

at the circle of creamy bubbles which formed on top of the steaming liquid.

"I hope Chantal realises how lucky she is!" I said with feeling.

"What is this about my being lucky?" Chantal sat down beside us.

"I was just saying to Peter that not many uncles would have given up their own hoilday for the sake of their niece!"

"Ah! But Peter is unique!" Chantal smiled across at him with affection. "In any case," she went on with youthful forthrightness, "it must be a novelty for him to have the company of a young woman who is not all starry-eyed when she looks at him! All my friends adore him. They think he is more wonderful than Dr. Kildare, Dr. Finlay and Dr. Casey all in one, and you should see the presents his women patients send him!"

"Chantal!" protested Peter, his cheeks tinged red with embarrassment.

"Well, it's true," she said cheerfully. "Combine the magic word 'doctor' with craggy good looks and pleasant manners and what can you expect?"

"Where has Carlo got to?" Peter hastily changed the subject, and I was glad, for in my delight at learning what his relationship to Chantal was, I had almost betrayed to Peter my own feelings for him, and now, more than ever after what Chantal had just been saying, I did not want to embarrass Peter by letting him think I was one more starry-eyed fan of his.

"Carlo had to attend to some business or

other," replied Chantal lightly, pouring herself a cup of coffee, "but he said he would be around later."

She looked across at me.

"What are your plans for today, Melanie?"

"I intend to do some sightseeing," I told her.

"That won't take the whole day, surely!" Chantal exclaimed. "I was hoping that you would be free to come shopping with me in the afternoon. Peter is hopeless as far as that is concerned."

"I would enjoy that!" I said with enthusiasm.

"Chantal," protested Peter, "you mustn't make a nuisance of yourself. Melanie may have other plans."

"I am not making a nuisance of myself!" she retorted. "It isn't fun shopping on one's own, and since Melanie is on her own, too, why shouldn't we go around together? You don't have a monopoly on her!" she added impudently.

I had to laugh, and Peter looked at me.

"I don't suppose it will be much fun sightseeing on one's own, either," he said slowly. "I haven't visited the Doge's Palace yet, although I should very much like to see it, so if you feel you can take pity on uncle as well as niece, Melanie, we could perhaps visit it together this morning?"

"Now, that is an idea!" said Chantal with delight. "If I don't have to look after Peter, I shall be free to go with Carlo to Florian's—if he hasn't made other arrangements meantime."

She seemed to take my acceptance of Peter's polite offer for granted as she continued:

"We could meet at the trattoria near the Wine Quay for lunch. You know the one, Peter. Alla Madonna. Then Melanie and I could go off on our shopping expedition from there."

Peter shook his head helplessly.

"You do like to arrange other people's lives for them, don't you, Chantal?"

She grinned with charming impudence.

"Why not? Someone has to do it, and it does seem to me utterly silly for us all to go off on our own, when we like each other, when there is nothing to stop us from going around together."

We finished breakfast, and glanced at the headlines of the English paper which Chantal had bought.

"EYE WITNESS TO THE KIDNAPPING!"

That was the banner headline which was spread over the front page, and which made my heart suddenly turn turtle.

Below the banner, there was a paragraph stating that a witness had come forward to tell the police that Lauren Radcliffe had been seen with two men in a gondola on the night of the kidnapping, and there was a possibility that this witness would be able to identify them.

"You know, Melanie," Peter looked at me thoughtfully, "it might not be a bad idea if you got away from the hotel as soon as possible this morning. I have the feeling that it will not be long before the reporters do their sleuthing and find out who the witness is.

"You may not have noticed, but the receptionist here has been eyeing you with a great deal of speculation since she came on duty a few minutes ago, and when she reads this report, and remembers that we put through a call to the Questura yesterday afternoon, in no time at all she will be trying to earn some money on the side by informing the newsmen of what she knows."

"Oh, no!" I looked at him, aghast. "I don't want a horde of reporters breathing down my neck again! Come on!" I stood up, impatient to be off. "I have everything I need with me, so let's get going!"

I turned to Chantal.

"If anyone, unless it is Captain Cerutti, asks where I am, you can say I have gone to the Lido for the day. That will keep them off our track!"

We hurried from the hotel along to the Piazzetta, and this time I took good care to keep in the cover of the lower arcade of the Doge's Palace, and not walk between St. Mark and St. Theodore. There seemed no point in tempting fate for a second time!

We spent the best part of the morning with another group of tourists in the great Palace of the Doges.

I was fascinated by it, there was so much to see. There was first of all the magnificent gateway, and the Scala d'Oro which led to the apartments of the Doges and the Council Chambers. There were the paintings of Veronesse and Bassano and Tintoretto, and particularly the remarkable paintings of Tintoretto and his pupils in the Sala del Maggior Consiglio, supposed to be one of the most imposing rooms in all Europe, and a room where much of Venice's history was made.

Peter was as interested in everything as I was, and we found ourselves looking wordlessly at each other from time to time as we found some particular feature or painting or piece of historical information which mutually appealed to us.

Indeed, it was amazing how often we liked the same things, and how often we caught each other's amused glance as the guide in his enthusiasm, muddled his English phrases with comic effect.

When we came to the climax of the tour, the visit to the pozzi or dungeons, and the Bridge of Sighs, although I knew there was as much fiction as fact in the guide's gruesome descriptions of what took place in the torture chamber, it seemed only natural that Peter should take my hand when I gave a shiver at one particularly ghoulish story.

When we came out from the cool, sunless interior of the great Palace to the brilliance of the noonday sun on the Piazza, I said to Peter:

"I don't think I could enjoy any more sightseeing today. I must have time to assimilate what I have already seen."

He glanced at his watch.

"It is too late for coffee and too early for our meeting with Chantal. How about filling in the rest of the morning by going to the top of the Campanile and admiring the view?"

We crossed the Square and took the lift to the

top of the great tower, along with a group of the tourists who had accompanied us round the Palace.

For about ten minutes we stood, leaning with our elbows on the parapet which surrounds the narrow viewing terrace, and looking down on Venice—to the midget shapes in the great square below, to the north, where the Clock Tower with its bronze Moors bestrides the entrance to the Mercerie, east to the domes and spires of St. Mark's and the white and pink bridal cake façade of the Palace we had recently visited, and south, out over the lagoon, to the blue, blue waters of the Adriatic.

It was as if I was looking down on a fairy island, but when the lift door opened, to debouch a fresh crowd of tourists, and Peter suddenly moved close to me, to guard me from being pushed too roughly against the balustrade by the crush, fairyland was here, at the top of the tower, in the warmth and closeness of his protective arms.

Chapter Seventeen

WE STOOD thus close for almost a minute, and I wondered if Peter was aware of the agitated fluttering of my heart as I was of his own strong heart beat. Then the press of tourists eased, and he drew away from me and said in a harsh voice:

"We shall make the lift if we hurry. If we don't go now, we could be late for our appointment with Chantal."

We just managed to squeeze into the lift as the door was about to close, and as we were carried downwards I stole a quick glance at Peter's face to see if he was as annoyed as his tone of voice suggested.

His mouth was no longer smiling, and his brow was creased in a frown, and I too frowned, wondering what had happened to cause his change of mood.

After we left the Campanile, I had great difficulty in keeping up with Peter as he went striding ahead of me across the Piazza towards the archway under the Clock Tower which leads to the Mercerie, and when a glance at the hour told me it was not yet noon, and since I reckoned that it could not take us an hour to walk from here to the restaurant where we were to meet Chantal, I came to the conclusion that

Peter had become bored with my company and was now anxious to get me off his hands and pass me over to his niece.

The feeling of bliss I had experienced since he had held me close at the top of the Campanile gave way to indignation.

I had not been the one who had suggested spending the morning together. He had. And he had also been perfectly happy to fall in with Chantal's plans for lunching together, so what had happened?

I hate being rushed along, especially past attractive-looking shops, and there were plenty of these in the Mercerie. I saw no reason why I should not stop to look at the goods displayed, even if I would no doubt be revisiting this area with Chantal later in the day.

Peter was about a couple of yards ahead of me when I paused to look at a particularly attractive painting in one of the windows, and he was not aware that I was no longer trying to keep up with him.

I stood in front of the shop and watched, with a feeling of malicious amusement, as he went striding on and disappeared from sight round the nearby corner.

Judging from his present mood, he would probably be furious with me when he realised that I was no longer with him, and I wondered if he would go on alone to the trattoria or retrace his steps to find out what had become of me.

I turned my attention to the goods in the window. There was a lovely little miniature which especially appealed to me, and as I stood trying to work out if I could afford to buy it, reflected in the glass of the window I noticed someone standing behind me.

I turned round quickly and found myself staring into Betty Lawrence's smiling face.

"I was so sure that it was you, Miss Lindsay, that I came across the road to speak to you." She gave a little sigh. "It is rather lonely in the hotel where I am now. All the other guests seem to be German or Scandinavian."

"I thought you were going home today?" I asked in surprise.

"I wish I was! Unfortunately, there has been some hold up with the funeral arrangements. There is always so much formality and red tape about police proceedings that I don't know where I am. I think it is because I am a foreigner that the authorities think they can push me around, and although I do speak Italian, they pretend to misunderstand me. It gets so infuriating!"

"What a pity your husband is not here to help you," I said sympathetically. "Have you no friends here in Venice you could turn to? How about—"

I stopped before I committed the faux pas of mentioning Carlo Benvenuto's name, but although I had not actually spoken of the devil, the words had been near enough my lips to conjure him up, because I saw Betty look over my shoulder and her strained expression changed to a smile of welcome.

"Carlo!" she exclaimed, and then went on

talking in a stream of what sounded to me like very fluent Italian, completely ignoring me as she gazed rapturously at the young man who had infatuated her.

Carlo's smile was bland and pleasant and he replied to her questions in Italian before turning to me with an odd look and saying: "I thought you were supposed to be sightseeing with Dr. Somerville this morning, signorina?"

"I was," I replied, "but now I am having a look at your lovely shops."

"Ah! I understand. The dottore is buying you a present in one of the shops and he has asked you to wait outside! I wondered what had happened when I saw you standing alone, since Chantal said that we were all going to meet for lunch at the trattoria Alla Madonna."

At his words, Betty Lawrence gave him a sharp glance and from the expression in her eyes, she was not at all pleased at this arrangement.

"I am not waiting for Peter," I informed Carlo. "As a matter of fact, I should not be at all surprised if he is at our rendezvous already. From the speed he was going when I last saw him, he is bound to be!" I smiled. "If you are on your way to the restaurant yourself, Carlo, you can tell him I won't be long!"

"I still do not understand." Carlo looked puzzled. "Are you telling me that Dr. Somerville walked off and left you on your own?" His eyes narrowed.

"A lover's tiff, no doubt!" Betty Lawrence,

displeased at the lack of attention Carlo was paying her, said acidly.

"One that I am glad of!" said Carlo gallantly. "Now I shall be able to help you with your shopping, signorina, and you should be glad, because now you will not be sold the goods at tourist prices!"

"I am only window shopping at the moment," I told him. "This afternoon Chantal and I will be back here to do our buying."

"Then this afternoon I shall still accompany you! Is it not fortunate for you that I am on leave at the moment?"

"I did not know that you were due leave, Carlo!" Betty Lawrence's words were more of a challenge than a statement. "You never said anything about leave to me!"

"The leave was unexpected, signora." Carlo turned his attention to her.

She said something in reply, but since she had again reverted to Italian, I had the feeling that she was deliberately excluding me from the conversation, so that they could make a tactful arrangement to meet later.

Certainly whatever Carlo said in answer must have pleased her, because by the time he had finished speaking she was looking very smug, and she was still smiling a secretive little smile as she said, "*Ciao*" to him, before turning to bid me a polite "Goodbye" as she left us to enter a shop on the other side of the Mercerie.

I smiled and shook my head at Carlo.

"Casanova could only have been an Italian!" I remarked. "Where else but in Italy would a man ask one girl out to lunch, offer to help another with her shopping, and obviously arrange to meet a third, all in the space of an hour or so?"

"I have to maintain the reputation of my countrymen!" he observed gravely, although for a moment there was amusement in the glance he gave me, but the amusement faded quickly as he continued:

"Signorina, I simply do not understand why Dr. Somerville walked off and left you on your own." He shook his head. "It was a strange thing to do!"

"We-ell, actually Peter didn't leave me," I had to confess. "It was more the other way about! You see," I went on to explain, "he was walking so quickly I could not keep up with him, and I was beginning to get fed up trailing after him and not getting a chance to look at the shops, so I lagged behind more and more, and he didn't even notice I wasn't with him! Then, when I stopped to have a look in this shop window, I saw him disappear round the corner, without even looking back to see if I was following! He possibly won't even notice that he is on his own until he gets to the trattoria!"

"That was a foolish move on your part, signorina!" Carlo's eyes narrowed. "Haven't you been—" he stopped short. "But what matter! I am with you now!" His voice perked up. "Come!" He took my arm. "Come with me!"

He urged me forward, and at the corner of the busy little shopping street we came face to face with a worried looking Peter.

"Melanie! What the devil do you mean by leaving me like that!" He looked angry and relieved at the same time. "How do you think I would have felt if anything had happened—"

"You have no need to worry about me!" I gave him a pert look. "Can't you see I am now under police protection?"

Carlo's fingers tightened spasmodically on my arm, and Peter looked completely taken aback.

"I met the signorina looking at the shops, dottore, and since we are all to meet there, I offered to accompany her to the trattoria."

"I am sorry you found my company boring, Melanie," said Peter in a bleak voice, "but at least you might have told me you were fed up, instead of letting me go off like that, not knowing you had stayed behind. I got the fright of my life when I missed you!"

"If you had been paying the slightest attention to me, you would have realised that you were walking far too quickly for me to keep up with you!" I replied with asperity. "You did not need to make it quite so obvious that you had had enough of my company!"

Carlo looked at our angry faces and smiled.

"I think the Signora Lawrence was right, non?" he said to me.

"No!" I exclaimed quickly, afraid that he would repeat her remark to Peter. "It is merely that Englishmen do not know how to treat a woman!"

Carlo was the only one of us who was in a good humour as we walked through the Mercerie and across the Rialto Bridge to the

Wine Quay, and I was still feeling so indignant with Peter that I noticed nothing of the busy, colourful streets through which we were passing.

Carlo and Chantal kept the conversation going at lunch time.

Peter and I only spoke to each other when necessity demanded that we should, and I felt utterly miserable at this new phase in our relationship. I picked disconsolately at the food set before me, and I was glad when the meal was eventually over, and Peter left us to go to get his car and drive to Padua for the afternoon.

In spite of Carlo's pleading that he be allowed to go shopping with us, Chantal told him point blank that she did not want him to join our expedition, because she had earlier proposed it as a girls only afternoon.

He looked most crestfallen, but Chantal was firm, and he eventually went off on his own, looking not at all pleased.

We strolled along the Ruga degli Orefici, and lingered to admire the market stalls, piled with glowing fruits and shining vegetables, and cheese stalls whose smell was somewhat overpowering. Even the fish shops here seemed much more interesting, and offered a much greater variety than their counterparts back home.

We ambled on across the Rialto Bridge, looking at the souvenirs on display on the sidewalks, and I was holding up a transparency of the Bridge, to see whether I wanted to buy it, or whether I could take a better photograph of it myself, when I thought I caught a glimpse of

Carlo lurking beside an umbrella stall a few yards behind us.

"Your admirer is still hopefully on our tail!" I whispered to Chantal, who looked round vaguely and said:

"Which admirer?"

I looked back with surprise at the umbrella stall, and there was no sight of Carlo there, or anywhere else in the vicinity. Yet once or twice, on our walk to the Mercerie, I had the curious feeling that there was someone following us, and one time I turned round quickly from staring in the window of a silk shop and could have sworn that it was Carlo's back I saw disappearing into a nearby bookshop.

I said nothing more to Chantal about him, but I was beginning to feel distinctly uneasy as we entered the glass showroom next to the Clock Tower in St. Mark's Square.

However, as we wandered from room to room in this fascinating shop, I soon forgot all about Carlo, or whoever it was who was dogging our footsteps, in my admiration of the fabulous colours and intricate craftsmanship of the glassware on display in the salons there.

One of the salesmen invited a group of prospective buyers to go and watch a display of glass blowing in the furnace room attached to the showroom, but Chantal was not interested, and said she would have another look round the shop instead, while I went with the others.

The furnace room was small and dark except for the glow from the oven. The guide explained to us the different processes involved, and we watched while one of the craftsmen created a superb golden pear.

My eyes were glued on the deft actions of the man, when someone tapped me on the shoulder.

"Isn't it fascinating?" With my eyes still dazzled from the furnace, I could not at first make out who the speaker was, and then I recognised Betty Lawrence.

"I could spend hours here," she went on. "In fact, I come here quite often, but it is nicer when there is someone you know to speak to!" She smiled at me. "May I join you?"

I hesitated. "Chantal is waiting for me in one of the display rooms," I said. "But certainly, if you are on your own, we could all have a coffee together."

"That is exactly what Chantal herself suggested!" said Mrs. Lawrence. "She got tired of waiting for you, and has gone across to Florian's to keep a table for us. She asked me to come and fetch you, since I knew where the furnace room was."

"Oh!" I was somewhat taken aback by Chantal's casual attitude.

"We had better get on our way before we interrupt the guide again," whispered Mrs. Lawrence. "This way."

"I am completely lost!" I said as we went down a narrow little stair. "There are so many odd little rooms and corridors in this place, it is like a maze!"

"Follow me!" ordered Mrs. Lawrence. "I have been here so often I could find my way blindfold!"

She led me along a short, narrow corridor, which I did not remember having traversed before, and out a side door into a narrow, shadowed lane, which was completely deserted.

She stood aside to let me pass her, and as I did so, I felt a sharp prick on my hip. I let out a startled exclamation and whirled around.

The whole world seemed to be spinning and as I staggered forward, Mrs. Lawrence put out a hand to steady me. As she did so, the light from the doorway from which we had emerged reflected on the unusually broad ring she was wearing on the little finger of her long, slim hand, and as I struggled to overthrow the awful feeling of lethargy which was possessing me, the reflection reminded me of another time, when the light from a window had shone down and illumined a similar ring, on the little finger of the unusually slim, long hand of a gondolier in black, and as I looked up, with diminishing awareness of Betty Lawrence's face, a trick of the light seemed to hood her with a black helmet, which emphasised her sharp features, and in that moment I recognised who she was and why she was so interested in me, and I tried to call out, but no words would come.

I felt fainter and fainter, and would have collapsed to the ground, but Betty Lawrence held my arm firmly and continued to propel me urgently forward up the fondamenta. As I struggled drunkenly over the uneven pathway, I thought I could hear the lapping of water, and then everything went blank.

Chapter Eighteen

WHEN I came to my senses, I was lying on a blanket on the floor of a small room. I tried to sit up, but my head ached and I felt sick when I moved, so I continued to lie there, gazing up at the ceiling and mentally reviewing my last minutes of consciousness.

It was hard to credit that Betty Lawrence was one of the kidnappers, but the more I thought about her, the more things dropped into place.

With hindsight, I realised that if I had not assumed right from the start that the gondolier was a man, I would have noticed the resemblance to Betty—the features, the long, slim woman's hands, even the betraying ring!

I shuddered as I remembered who else had looked down on the gondola that night, and, even more clearly than I, seen that gondolier. It had been someone who, unlike me, had not been deceived by the sexless figure in the black rubber suit. Someone who knew the gondolier too well to be mistaken—Alice Sinclair!

Oh, yes. Alice had recognised Betty all right. She had even called to her by the name she used for her, "Sis." I had mistaken her shout for a hiss of surprise when the beetles had flown in at

her. And, of course, there could have been no
doubt that Betty had also seen and heard and
recognised her sister at the window, and known
that Alice was sure to talk about the event and
wonder at Betty's actions. Also, as a New
Yorker, there was the danger of her having
recognised one of its leading socialites—Lauren
Radcliffe.

Mrs. Lawrence knew, too, that she had gone
too far with the kidnapping to give up now, so
she had to act.

I shivered again and, pulling the blanket
round me, I sat up, hugging my knees.

What had gone on in Alice Sinclair's room less
than an hour after that gondola had passed
beneath her window?

Had her step-sister gone to her, after delivering Lauren to this house in which I too was now
being held prisoner, and had she tried at first to
buy her silence? Had she offered Alice a share of
the ransom money, and had this offer been
refused?

And whose hand had driven the deadly dagger
between Alice Sinclair's narrow shoulder blades?
Had Betty herself murdered her sister, or had it
been her partner-in-crime, whoever he was, who
had driven the weapon home?

And why hadn't they taken the precaution of
making sure that the blow had been instantly
fatal? Had they been too busy ransacking the
room, faking evidence to point to theft, to check,
or had my movements as I got from bed in the
room next door, put them to flight before they
could make sure they had killed her? Had they

even thought I had spotted them when they made their escape, as I came along the corridor to find out what had happened?

Had Eduardo Conti been the other man? But no, he had been too slight for that, so where did he fit in?

I crouched on my blanket, trying to fix the pieces together.

How shocked Betty must have been when she realised that her sister had still been alive when I had found her, but she had been quickwitted enough to make so much fuss when she had seen me kneeling over the body to drown out the dying woman's words, words which would have betrayed her, had I not misinterpreted them.

It had been so easy to think Alice had whispered, "A man, and gone to leave—assist—" when even now, as my mouth reformed the sounds, I heard myself saying, "A man and gondolier, my sister—"

Yes. It was small wonder Betty Lawrence had wanted to get rid of me. Cerutti had said that Conti was a thug who would commit any crime for money. Betty must also have known this, and hired him, with the jewels she had stolen from her sister, to kill me in order to get rid of another unwanted witness.

But how had a woman like Betty Lawrence known how to get in touch with a criminal like Conti?

For some reason I thought of Carlo Benvenuto, a policeman with a knowledge of crime and criminals; a man who had been following me surreptitiously all that day; a man who, from the way he dressed and spoke, liked the good things in life; a man who had had, and was possibly still having, an affair with Alice Sinclair's sister!

These two must have been more than ever anxious to get rid of me when they heard, as Carlo was bound to have heard, that I had actually seen Lauren Radcliffe in the gondola, and might at any moment realise who the gondolier had been!

I remembered how they had met that very morning in the Mercerie, and talked to each other in Italian, ignoring me. Had they, at that moment, with ghoulish humour, been discussing my fate in my very presence?

I felt ill. If Betty had had no compunction in killing her own sister, she would have even less compunction now in getting rid of me, when I knew so much more about her activities!

I shivered as if with ague, wondering how soon she would return with her executioner to perform the job. Then, the instinct of self-preservation came to my aid.

In a fury I struggled to my feet, dropping the blanket to the floor. I was damned if I was just going to wait here, for her to act!

I took quick stock of the room I was in. It was very small, and lit by a small bulb which dangled on a thin cord from the ceiling, and was completely unfurnished. The only covering on the bare boards of the floor was the grey blanket at my feet. The place smelt of disuse and mice, and cobwebs hung from the ceiling and across the corners, and curtained off the one small window, which was shuttered over from the outside.

The ceiling came down so low at the window side that I surmised I must be in an attic room of the building. I had to stoop as I crossed to the window to try and peer out, but the bar which closed the window was rusted into position, and my fingers were still too weak and shaky to try to force it open, to get to the shutter outside.

I went to try the door, in some foolish hope that it might have been left unlocked, but I was wasting my time, so I went back to the window.

If only there was something with which I could lever the bolt. I bit my lip in thought as I gazed round the bare room. Even my handbag had been taken from me, so that I had neither a comb nor a file, not even a metal coin with which to prise the hasp.

In my frustration, I went back to the door and started to kick at it and hammer on it with my fists, but the noise that I made was drowned out by the reverberating clangour of a great bell which made the shutter rattle and sent the mice behind the wainscotting skittering in fright up and down inside the walls.

I stopped my hammering to listen to the sound of the bell from the clock tower, which, judging from the volume of sound, must be quite close at hand.

When I had wakened, I had had no idea of the time, nor of how long I had been unconscious. The glass on the face of my watch had been broken, possibly when I had been dumped on the floor, and the hour hand had jammed, although the mechanism still ticked merrily on.

I counted each reverberating clang from one to nine. So it was nine o'clock, but nine at night or nine in the morning? At very least I had been here for five hours, and I had no doubt that at this moment all over the city the carabinieri and my friends would be searching for me, as they had already searched in vain for the other girl Betty Lawrence and her accomplice had kidnapped.

I rattled once more with desperation at the window hasp. I simply had to get away from here before Betty could return with Carlo.

Cold sweat dripped down my back, and terror lent strength to my fingers as I tugged desperately at that rusted metal bolt. Finally, my fingers bruised and bleeding with the effort, I managed to pull it from its socket, and open the window, but the wooden shutter on the outside had been nailed tightly shut with uneven board, and I gazed at it with tears of helplessness in my eyes.

But I couldn't give up now, I thought determinedly, and I shoved my fingers through the space between the boards and pulled and pulled. My fingers ached with pain, and only desperation kept me struggling on.

Then, when I had almost given up hope, the damp, rotting wood suddenly gave way, catapulting me back across the room when I made the final successful wrench, so that I stumbled and sat heavily down on the floor, but hope eased the pain of the fall.

I struggled once more to my feet, and resumed my efforts. If one board could give, so could the other! I tore wildly at it, using all the strength of my new-found hope, and then I uttered a cry of triumph when at last this board too gave way, and I was able to open the shutter and look out of the window.

It was night time. Below me, water reflected the light of an occasional lamp on the narrow fondamenta below, and across the rio, the rooftops were outlined against the dull red, reflected glow of the city lights on the low cloud.

The attic window opened on to gently sloping tiles, which stopped at a broad parapet which ran the length of the building. Gingerly I edged through the window. The ragged wood that remained from the boards I had ripped away caught at my dress, tearing the skirt, but what did clothes matter at a time like this!

I clung with my aching hands to the sill as I pulled myself through the narrow aperture, and then, blessing the fact that I had been wearing my flat walking shoes for shopping and sightseeing that day, a day which now seemed almost a lifetime ago, I clambered slowly and carefully to the edge of the roof and leaned against the parapet.

From here I surveyed the situation.

The house appeared to be about three storeys high and there were no handy pipes at this side down which I could slide to the ground. However, the parapet led to the roof of a neighbouring house, which was almost a storey lower than the one I was on, and which had balconies at every window right to the ground.

In shadow cast up by the lights along the ing it that elongated, waxen effect I had seen along the parapet until I was overlooking the building next to mine. The nearest balcony was about six feet below me, shadowly outlined, and I tried to nerve myself for the jump, but I was shaking so much with my recent efforts, I could not find the courage, and I simply stood there, looking stupidly down at the narrow strip of balcony.

As I stood there, a motorboat glided up the canal and stopped at the landing place of the house on whose roof I perched.

A woman climbed from it on to the landing steps, and the boat started up and went phut-phutting away along the rio. The light above the landing place fell full on the woman's face, giv-glow in the sky to guide me, I groped my way edge of the rio, but with enough light from the once before, as Betty Lawrence came hurrying towards the entrance of the house on whose roof tiles my feet seemed riveted.

Any moment now she would come up to the attic, and find me gone. Any moment now she would look out of the window through which I had made my escape, and see me standing here, helplessly, on the very edge of the roof.

One shove, one energetic poke with a long-handled broom from that window, and I would be sent crashing down to the narrow stone walk below.

Like Eduardo Conti, whose usefulness, with

his recognition by Cerutti, had come to an end, making him one more possible witness for the prosecution, I would then be rolled into the dark rio, to drown among the orange peel and the oil cans and the dead rats which I had occasionally seen drift past on the water.

I tensed myself for a final effort, and jumped desperately to the balcony below. I was sure the clangour of my landing must have been heard in all Venice, but no one came to the window to investigate, and, with frightened urgency, I somehow managed to manœuvre from balcony to lower balcony, the tears of relief coursing down my cheeks as I made the final drop to the ground and went staggering down the narrow way which led to the brightness of a well-lit street about a couple of hundred feet away.

I had almost reached the junction when Carlo Benvenuto came striding round the corner.

He stopped dead in amazement at sight of me, and let out a shout.

I screamed and pushed him violently aside as I fled into the ruga, elbowing my way through the groups of well-dressed tourists who were staring at the brightly-lit shop windows, and who turned to stare after me as if I was a mad woman.

I thought I heard the sound of feet chasing after me, and I literally flung myself into the surprised arms of a grey-uniformed policeman who was standing outside one of the shops.

Clinging to his arm, I demanded hysterically to be taken at once to Captain Cerutti at the Questura.

While most of my speech must have been quite incomprehensible to him, the magic words Cerutti and Questura were the open sesame for action.

Taking my arm in a tight grip, he hastily escorted me down the ruga into a street I recognised as the Mercerie, and out into the Piazza, to where a group of carabinieri were standing.

There were startled exclamations, and excited voices were raised in questions, as my guide pointed back along the way we had come. Then, while three of the men followed him back towards the ruga, the other two guided me along the piazzetta on the north side of San Marco, to where a police launch was drawn up at the landing stage of a small canal. Here there was more excited chattering to the man in charge, and then I was helped aboard, and taken to the Questura.

Chapter Nineteen

I was taken directly to Captain Cerutti's private office where the worried-looking police captain's face cleared with delighted surprise the moment he saw me.

"Signorina Lindsay!" He sprang up from behind his desk and came forward to shake me warmly by the hand.

Then came the explanations. The questions. The answers. The hustle of activity as more senior officers came to the room to talk with me, and more carabinieri were dispatched to the building near the Clock Tower where I had been taken by Betty Lawrence.

After what seemed hours of non-stop questions and answers, I felt my head spinning.

Cerutti sent for coffee and brandy to revive me, so that I could make a final coherent statement of what had happened before I was free to go.

Even then, seeing how shaken I still was, instead of letting me leave right away, he ordered everyone from his room and told me to sit there quietly for a time.

"I shall send for the Signor Ferguson to take you back to your hotel, signorina," he decided.

"I expect you would like to be with a friend at a time like this, wouldn't you?"

He stopped talking to answer a knocking on the door. When he opened it, an excited conversation ensued, and Cerutti turned back to me, looking very pleased with events.

"We have found the Signorina Radcliffe, unharmed, in a room next to the one from which you escaped!" he told me exultantly. "She is being brought to the station now, so if you will excuse me," he bowed and clicked his heels, "I shall go to meet her. Your friend Signor Ferguson will soon be here to take you home," he added reassuringly.

Indeed, Ben arrived as Cerutti was taking his leave. They exchanged some words in Italian, and I thought I heard Ben ask for a doctor, whereupon Cerutti turned back to look at me, then nodded his head with a puzzled smile and departed.

Ben closed the door behind him and looked across at me. His face still showed signs of strain, but the smile he greeted me with was bright and happy.

"Thank God you are safe, my dear. I would never have forgiven myself if anything had happened to you. It would have been my fault, you see, for acquiescing to Cerutti's scheme."

I gaped at him.

"What do you mean?"

He came and sat on the desk near me, looking down at me. "First of all, let me tell you that Betty Lawrence has been caught in the building you escaped from, before she could do further mischief. Harry Lawrence was arrested on his arrival at Mestre, on his way to join his wife, and they are both being charged with kidnapping, murder and a few other lesser crimes."

He took a cigarette from the packet he had taken from his pocket and lit it with a hand which was still shaking slightly. "They are rather nasty, stop-at-nothing characters, the pair of them, and they deserve each other, as well as what fate now has in store for them!"

"But I don't understand!" I gawked at him in bewilderment. "How is Harry Lawrence involved in all this?"

Ben seemed surprised at my question.

"Hadn't you realised he was the brains behind the affair? Who did you think was her accomplice?"

I shook my head stupidly.

"Where does Carlo fit in?"

"Carlo?" repeated Ben frowning. "Carlo Benvenuto?"

I nodded. "Yes, he was one of the gang, wasn't he?"

Ben began to laugh. "Carlo? Good heavens, no! Poor Carlo would be annoyed if he ever thought you could suspect him of such dastardly actions! Especially," he continued more soberly, "when he had been your faithful watchdog for almost forty-eight hours non stop!

"You see, his 'sick leave' was merely an excuse to let him pretend to squire you, or be in your company as much as possible. Being on friendly terms with young Chantal was a great help in this.

"After Cerutti knew that both you and Alice Sinclair had seen the kidnappers, he deduced why Alice had been killed, and why Eduardo Conti had been trying to kill you, too.

"From the moment you told him about seeing that gondola, he put you under surveillance, but not too close surveillance, because he did not want the kidnappers to realise you were being watched. He had an idea they might try to get at you again, as I gathered from Chantal they had tried the other morning in the Piazzale Roma, and Cerutti wanted to catch them out in the attempt and so find out who they were!"

"You mean, he was using me as bait!" I exclaimed indignantly.

Ben looked shamefaced.

"We all thought it a workable idea, except Peter. He didn't like it at all, and thought that you should be told about it. However, Cerutti thought you might give the game away without meaning to, of course, and he deputed either Peter or I to be with you at all times, as unofficial watchdogs. Carlo and another officer were always within shouting distance, and there were also some innocent 'tourists' on hand if trouble started.

"Poor Peter, he didn't half get hauled over the coals for letting you out of his sight this morning!"

"That was really my fault!" I excused Peter quickly and Ben gave an odd smile at this, before going on with his story.

"We all got hauled over the coals for what happened at the glass showrooms this afternoon, but that was one of those things we could not foresee.

"From what you had said to her when she had met you in the Mercerie this morning, Betty Lawrence knew that you were coming back to do shopping in this area, and she gambled on the fact that you would be attracted, as every tourist is, to Gino Cenedese's, both to look round his wonderful showrooms and to watch the glass blowing.

"She must have spent most of the afternoon lurking around the place, but because she was such a frequent visitor in more innocent times, no one there paid much attention to her.

"Fortunately, the guide in the furnace room did happen to notice you leave with a tall woman, and when, after your disappearance became known, he was questioned by Carlo, who had actually been waiting outside the shop, and described the woman, Carlo instantly recognised who it might be.

"There was no real proof that it was Betty Lawrence, but the coincidence was too much to be overlooked.

"Cerutti had the Lawrences investigated, and Carlo was directed to keep the date which Betty had impudently made with him for the early part of the evening, before her husband was due back from Milan!

"I think it amused her to think how she was thumbing her nose at the police, but she was far from amused when she learned that it was this date which led Carlo to you and the house where she had been holding Lauren Radcliffe!

"When you went charging past him, he was glad to know you had escaped. but he also realised he would have to go in after Mrs. Lawrence before she did Lauren any harm." He paused for breath.

"I can hardly believe it all happened! I am sure I shall wake up and find it has been a bad dream!" I shivered and took another sip of brandy.

"Ben, do the Lawrences already have a criminal record?" I asked as he lit a fresh cigarette.

He shook his head. "No, otherwise Cerutti might have got on to them earlier. However, inquiries turned up several things. For example, Lawrence had some connection with the Mafia in the States before coming here, although he had not been engaged in criminal activities, to their knowledge.

"In Milan he has the reputation of being a hard business man, quite unscrupulous in some of his dealings. He had built up his uncle's chemical firm from nothing to a flourishing concern by methods which were on the borderline of honesty. Anyone who got in his way he got rid of. He had, in fact, achieved his ambition of making his uncle's concern one of the top ones in Italy, when Radcliffe came along to make a bid for one of his rivals. This merger would have put Lawrence almost right back to where he had started, because he had little actual capital behind him, and he was determined this would not happen.

"Inspired by the current crop of political kidnappings, he saw a clever way out of his dilemma.

"If Radcliffe did not have the money for the take-over there could be no merger, so Lawrence decided to see to it that the money would not be there!"

"You mean, that getting together the ransom money demanded for his daughter would put Radcliffe out of business?"

"Yes. What is more, with that money, Lawrence intended to buy over the company Radcliffe had been after! He was a crafty devil, and entirely without moral scruples, and his wife was with him every step of the way. They were two of a kind, and if anything, Betty was the worse, because she even agreed to having her own sister killed when she thought that Alice would betray them!"

I looked at him with a shudder. "So I was right about a lot of the things I guessed at?"

"Yes," said Ben grimly, "even to realising that once the money was paid, neither you nor Lauren could be allowed to live because you knew who your kidnappers were!

I started to tremble, and Ben put a comforting arm around me.

"It is all over now, Melanie. Try to forget about it. Remember that now the only men who will be trailing after you will be the local wolves! You can really begin to enjoy your holiday now!"

"Yes!" I agreed with a glad sigh. "And now that you have written up the Radcliffe story, you will surely be free to show me a little more of Venice?" I asked hopefully.

Ben shook his head.

"I am sorry, my dear, but that is out of the question. The Radcliffe story has been written up, it is true, but I have had word of interesting developments elsewhere."

He stood up.

"Tomorrow, Melanie, I am off to Tangier to follow this new lead."

"To Tangier!" I echoed. "Oh, Ben! You can't go off just like that! Venice won't be the same without you! I might as well pack up and go home myself!"

I sat upright and looked at him.

"It's true, you know. I am sure I could not stay on here on my own now. There would be too many ghosts!" I shivered. "Oh, Ben!" I stared at him forlornly. "I wish I had never come to Venice!"

Ben was standing at the window, looking down on the now moonlit rio. At my words he turned to me, smiling.

"Do you really wish that, Melanie? Do you really?" He looked at me speculatively. "You know, if you hadn't come here, you would never have met Peter Somerville!"

My cheeks flooded with colour.

"What do you mean?" I asked shakily.

His smile was half amused, half sad.

"My dear, I have watched you two when you are together. I have seen the look in your eyes when he is with you, as if no one else in the whole world existed. When he speaks to you, I know this sounds foolish, but there is a glow about you, an aura of happiness!"

"Don't be silly!" I snapped, furious at having made my feelings for Peter so obvious. "I have only known him a few days!"

"Sometimes to the lucky ones, it happens just like that."

He came over to where I was sitting and looked down at me, ruffling my hair with an affectionate hand.

"I think you are one of the lucky ones, Melanie," he said softly.

"I wish I was!" I could not keep the sadness from my voice. "But Peter has not much time for me, for some reason. Haven't you heard how he walked off and left me this morning?"

"Yes, I heard. Peter told me himself. He was angry about it."

He bent down and kissed my forehead. "Stop worrying, Melanie. Things will work out." He ruffled my hair once more.

"*Ciao*, my dear. I shall send you a postcard from Tangier!"

He crossed to the door and opened it, and there was laughter in his voice as he turned to me once more and said: "Here is the doctor for you, Melanie."

The door closed behind him, and I looked up, and saw Peter Somerville standing with his back to it.

"Melanie!"

He was across the room in two strides.

I stood up, facing him.

He caught hold of both my hands and looked

down at me. "Ben said you needed me. My dear love, are you all right?"

I looked at him, colour flooding my cheeks at his words.

"What did you say, Peter?" I whispered.

His hand gripped mine so tightly I thought he would break my bones.

"I should never have gone to Padua this afternoon. I should have stayed at your side all the time, and yet I could not," he groaned. "I was afraid you would see how foolish I was about you."

"Peter!" I was trembling as I clung to his hands. "You called me your dear love!" I laughed shakily. "Do you speak like that to all your women patients?" I stared up at him, lips parted in a smile.

"No!" he said explosively. "And you are not, and never will be a patient of mine!"

He released my hands and put one arm round me, drawing me close, while with his free hand he tilted my chin so that for a long moment I looked up into his eyes, and then he kissed me, not as Ben had ever kissed me, not as anyone else had ever kissed me, until my mouth felt bruised, and I could no longer breathe, and then he let me go, and said almost angrily:

"That is why you can never be a patient of mine. They can send for some other doctor to attend to you!"

His hand was on the handle of the door, turning it, ready to leave, when I recovered my senses enough to call out to him.

"No, Peter, no!" I ran to him, and put my

hand on his arm. "Ben did not send for you because you were a doctor!" I was laughing at him, so happy, so grateful to Ben, because it was Ben, and his postcard, which had brought me to this moment, to this place in Venice, to meet my love. And even before I had, Ben had realised what was happening.

"Ben sent for you, Peter, because he is a very perceptive friend of mine!"

I pulled him round to face me.

"Don't leave me, Peter. We have so much to learn still about each other, so much to talk over together, and a whole wonderful week still, here in Venice, to do our learning and our talking!"

He looked down at me, eyes widening in growing understanding, beginning to glow with delight.

Boldly I put my hands on his shoulders, and stood on tip-toe to touch his lips with mine, as I whispered the words which were to start our new relationship:

"Hello, my love!"